elixir

eli

HILARY DUFF

with ELISE ALLEN

SIMON & SCHUSTER BFYR

NEW YORK LONDON TORONTO SYDNEY

An imprint of Simon & Schuster Children's Publishing Division
1230 Avenue of the Americas, New York, New York 10020

For information about special discounts for bulk purchases,
please contact Simon & Schuster Special Sales at 1-866-506-1949
or business@simonandschuster.com.
The Simon & Schuster Speakers Bureau can bring authors to
your live event. For more information or to book an event, contact
the Simon & Schuster Speakers Bureau at 1-866-248-3049
or visit our website at www.simonspeakers.com.
Book design by Lizzy Bromley
The text for this book is set in Cochin and OL Hairline Gothic.
Manufactured in the United States of America
2 4 6 8 10 9 7 5 3 1
Library of Congress Cataloging-in-Publication Data
Duff, Hilary, 1987–
Elixir / Hilary Duff with Elise Allen. — 1st ed.
p. cm.
Summary: Clea Raymond, a talented young photojournalist
who has spent her life in the spotlight, and her best friends, Rayna and Ben,
travel the globe trying to unravel a centuries-old
mystery that could reveal her soulmate's identity and the secret of her
father's disappearance.
ISBN 978-1-4424-0853-1 (hardcover)
[1. Mystery and detective stories. 2. Photojournalism—Fiction.
3. Supernatural—Fiction. 4. Voyages and travels—Fiction.
5. Celebrities—Fiction. 6. Youths' writings.] I. Allen, Elise.
II. Title.
PZ7.D8713Eli 2010
[Fic]—dc22
2010022053
ISBN 978-1-4424-0859-6 (eBook)

In dreams

AND

in love

THERE ARE

no impossibilities.

one

I COULDN'T BREATHE.

Wedged in the middle of an ocean of people, I gasped for air, but nothing came. The heat from a million writhing bodies radiated over me, their sweat weighing down the air. I searched anxiously for an escape, but painfully bright lights strobed on and off, clouding my sense of direction.

I was losing it. I was going to pass out.

I forced in a deep breath and tried to talk myself down. I was fine. It wasn't like I was anywhere dangerous. I was on a dance floor, in the most exclusive nightclub in Paris. People lined up all night in the freezing cold for even a chance to stand where I was now.

It didn't help. The techno beat thrummed into my brain, five notes repeating over and over and over until I knew I'd have to scream. The crowd pushed even closer and I couldn't move my arms, could barely turn my head, and I had a sudden vision of this being forever, an eternity packed in this tiny space as confining as a coffin.

Like my father's coffin. Did he have a coffin? Was he even buried? Did anyone even know when he died? Was he alone, lost in the jungle? Was he attacked by animals? Was he found and tortured? Had he prayed for us to save him before it was too late?

That did it. Now I was hyperventilating. I closed my eyes and forced my arms up and apart, swimming for dear life through layers of writhing, grinding bodies. I nearly cried when I felt a burst of winter air on my face. I'd made it out to the balcony. I staggered to an open love seat and leaned against its back as I drank in gulp after gulp of fresh air.

I was back; I was okay. I took another deep breath, this one calm and centering, and looked out over the nighttime Paris skyline, the Eiffel

Tower bathed in yellow lights. It was beautiful. Automatically I reached for the camera bag dangling at my hip, but of course I hadn't brought it to the club. I sighed and let my hand drift to the silver iris charm I always wore around my neck. I ran my fingers over its three upright petals and three drooping sepals. *The petals represent faith, valor, and wisdom,* my dad had said when he fastened the necklace around my neck on my fifth birthday. *You already have all those things in spades, little girl,* he'd continued, then knelt down to look me straight in the eye. *But when things get tough and you forget, this necklace can remind you.*

"Clea? Are you okay?"

I smiled and turned to see my best friend since forever clicking across the balcony in high strappy sandals. Those combined with her golden dress, endless legs, and thick mane of red curls made Rayna look like she'd stepped out of a Greek myth.

"I'm fine," I assured her, but the sudden crease between her eyes proved she didn't quite believe me.

"You were thinking about him?"

I didn't have to answer. Her eyes fell to my hand, still fingering the iris charm, and she knew.

"It's worse when you don't sleep," she said. "Maybe we should go back to the room and . . ."

I shook my head before she could finish. I actually felt a lot better. And even if I didn't, sleep wouldn't help. More often than not in the past year, sleep was just an invitation to nightmares I didn't want.

Besides, even though I knew Rayna would leave in a heartbeat if I asked her, I also knew it was the last thing in the world she wanted to do. She had only three days before winter break ended and she had to go back to Vallera Academy in Connecticut to finish up her senior year. I knew what that was like; this time last year I was at Vallera with her. It took an extreme act of pleading on my part to get my mom to agree to the homeschool switch. Rayna and I had dedicated the entire three-week vacation to traveling and jet-setting, and there was no way she wanted to lose a single second of her remaining time to something as mundane as hanging out in a hotel room.

"I'm great," I assured her. "I just needed a break. And Le Féroce is open all night; we're just getting started."

"Yes!" Rayna squealed. Then she leaned in close and added meaningfully, "I'll fetch our dates."

I grinned as she clicked back to the glass doors. Our "dates." I loved that she called them that when we'd only met them an hour ago at the bar.

I settled into the love seat and looked back out at the skyline, composing photos in my mind and musing about assignments I might take when I got home. Something meaningful, I hoped. Maybe something that could feature GloboReach, my dad's charitable foundation. So much of my dad's press in his last year centered around the vials he uncovered; it's like the world forgot he dedicated himself to more important things, like saving people's lives.

"Enter . . . the boys!" Rayna proclaimed with a flourish as she arrived with "our dates" in tow. "Pierre . . . and Joseph."

"Hi." I smiled, taking the drink Joseph offered me. "Thanks."

"Pas de problème," Pierre answered for Joseph as he collapsed into the cushioned chair next to mine. "It is a pleasure to take care of *deux belles filles* like yourselves." He placed two drinks on a small table, then cried out to Rayna, *"Viens, ma cherie! Viens!"*

With a playful growl, he wrapped his arms around Rayna's waist and pulled her down on his lap. Was he for real? Rayna seemed to think so. She squealed happily, then settled in sidesaddle.

"You are very bad indeed," she scolded him.

"Mais non!" he protested, then handed her a drink as a peace offering. *"Pour toi."*

"Merci," Rayna replied, locking eyes with Pierre and arching her back just enough to add another cup size as she took a sip, then set her glass back down. *"Et pour toi,"* she purred, and closed the distance between them for a long, involved kiss.

Fascinating. Thanks to my parents, I've been lucky enough to see some of the greatest actors of our time perform onstage. Rayna engaging in the art of seduction beat all of them, hands down. I wasn't sure about her choice of partner this time, though. Pierre was so beautiful, it would be a crime against humanity for him not to be a male model, but he was so slim and angular that I imagined sitting on his lap and kissing him would be like cuddling with a porcupine. Rayna didn't seem to mind. She came up for air with a smile that promised more, then leaned toward me and stage-whispered, "Pierre and I are *soulmates*."

I tried not to laugh. I would have if it was just a line, if she were just saying it to assure Pierre he wasn't spending his drink money in vain. But I knew in this moment, Rayna absolutely meant it, as strongly as she had meant it when she'd said it about Alexei, Julien, Rick, Janko, Steve, and Avi . . . all of whom she had fallen head over heels with in the past three weeks.

Personally, I don't believe in soulmates. Rayna relishes the concept. She adores the breathless romance of a brand-new relationship. It's a drug for her; nothing makes her feel more alive. And each time that whirlwind of ecstasy sweeps her away, she truly believes that *this* time it's real; this time it's forever. No matter how often she's let down and disappointed, Rayna remains endlessly optimistic about the prospect of true love. It's an attitude I can't relate to at all, but in her I admire it to no end.

"I'm happy for you," I said. And I meant it. If a fantasy about the man with the angles brought her joy, I was all for it.

She returned my smile, then went back to kissing Pierre, expertly avoiding getting impaled on the points of his chin and cheekbones.

"Ahem."

Joseph had perched on the love seat next to me. His brow was furrowed. Poor guy probably assumed he'd have my full attention the moment he arrived.

"Sorry," I offered, turning my body to face him.

"Are you okay?" he asked in a clipped British accent. "You looked terribly upset when you left the dance floor."

"I did?" I had a disturbing image of a juicy Page Six headline: Senator Victoria Weston's Daughter Loses It in Paris Nightclub. "Did people notice?"

"In the middle of that zoo?" He laughed. "No one but the three of us. Or the two of us, really. I'm not sure Pierre's had his eyes off your friend's . . ." He tried gesturing with his face to illustrate Pierre's obsession with Rayna's chest, but it was impossible to do so without stepping all over his refined sense of manners.

It was pretty adorable, really. "It's okay," I assured him, "I know what you mean."

"Oh thank goodness," he gushed. And as we laughed together, I wondered if I shouldn't reconsider Joseph. I had written him off as Pierre's wingman, but maybe that wasn't fair. Physically I had no complaints: He was a little taller than my five-four, with pale skin and dark hair, a forelock of which constantly threatened to fall into his face. He was slim, but clearly toned and strong, like . . .

"Do you play soccer?" I asked. "You look like a soccer player."

Great. Now I sounded as cheesy as his friend Pierre. "I mean—"

"No, it's okay. I *do* play soccer, actually. Not professionally or anything, but . . ."

Joseph started to tell me about himself, and I did listen, but I also watched his eyes.

The eyes are the windows to the soul, Clea. My father began telling me that when I was very young, and by the time I was old enough to know it was a cliché, it already felt like an eternal truth.

Joseph's eyes were powder blue, open and clear. A little too clear, to be honest. I kept waiting for something he said to light a fire in them, but it never happened. When he told me he was in the middle of a two-year sabbatical to "travel the world and find his passions," I knew I was done. The right guy for me is someone who lives his passions, not someone on a scavenger hunt to find them. Rayna would say that didn't matter; Joseph didn't have to be my dream man to be a wonderful night's entertainment. Maybe she was right, but I got exhausted just thinking about all the energy it would take to seem interested when I really wasn't.

Joseph leaned forward so his forelock fell over his brow. "So now that I've told you everything there is to know about me . . . tell me about yourself, Clea Raymond."

"Actually . . . I'd like to go upstairs and dance," I answered honestly.

"Great, let's do it," he replied, but I shook my head as he started to rise.

"That's okay," I said with what I hoped was a kind enough smile. "I really just want to be by myself for a little."

"Are you sure?"

"Yeah . . . you don't have to wait for me or anything. I don't want to waste your night. There are a lot of other girls in the club. "

"Ah," he said, rising.

I cringed—had I hurt his feelings? Then he smiled. He may not have been happy, but he got it.

"Well then . . . nice meeting you." He extended his hand, and I shook it. He was a sweet guy; I hoped he'd find someone else. As he strode back inside, I tapped Rayna on the shoulder and caught her eye, then made my way upstairs. The breeze kicked up as I walked, and I shivered. My strappy silk cocktail dress was far too skimpy for winter—even a winter buffered by the club's powerful heat lamps—but it was perfect for dancing. Not the claustrophobic mosh-fest nightmare going on in the main club, but *dancing*.

I pulled open the balcony doors and immediately felt at ease. Le Féroce's small Upper Lounge was the polar opposite of its wild downstairs, and far more my style. It was intimate, with subtle lighting, plush booths, candlelit sconces, a large mahogany bar, a dance floor, and a small stage on which a phenomenal singer belted out Etta James. I felt embraced by the whole atmosphere, and threaded my way through the other dancers until I was right in front of the stage, where I let the music carry me away.

I love dancing. If the music's right, I get lost in it, and for a little while I can forget about everything else. Dancing for me is what I imagine yoga or meditation is for Rayna. It's similar to how I feel when I'm rock climbing, all by myself on a cliff side where I can only concentrate on the next handhold, the next foothold, and the addictive pain in my muscles as I pull myself higher and higher.

My mind wandered as I danced, and I found myself imagining how the conversation would have continued with Joseph. He gave me the big clue by calling me by my full name. Based on experience, that meant there was a good chance his next question would have been, "So . . . what's it like being Victoria Weston's daughter?"

It was a crazy question, especially coming from someone like Joseph, who had casually mentioned his ties to the throne and his family's regular appearance in the British tabs. He knew what it was like to live in the spotlight. But he wouldn't have been asking to really find out the answer, just for something to say.

Rayna loved that question. She got it all the time too, only her version asked what it was like to be *connected* to the Weston family. It was the perfect setup. She'd answer by locking eyes with the guy who asked and cooing meaningfully, "It's the people. I get to meet the most incredible people. . . ."

That was never my answer. I am not a people person. Maybe that's why I was so okay with homeschooling my senior year. Rayna said she could never do it. She'd be plagued by the dozens of social dramas she'd miss every day. I wasn't bothered by that in the least. It's not that I don't like people; there are certain people I absolutely couldn't live without. Or at least people I *feel* I couldn't live without. I've learned this year that the truth is I can't live *well* without certain people, but I can live.

Rayna is one of those people. I've known her all my life—Rayna's mother Wanda is my mother's "Equine Professional." Basically, Wanda's the nanny for my mother's horses. It's a full-time job, and Wanda could never do it if she had to commute. Instead she has a guesthouse on the property, where she's always lived with Rayna's dad, George.

Mom and Wanda were pregnant at the exact same time, and Dad told me it drove him crazy because neither of them would listen to him and take it easy. At nine months pregnant and big as a house, Wanda would still waddle endlessly around the property, mucking stalls, scooping grain, and personally grooming and walking every horse. Mom was in state politics back then, and even though most of her travel was fairly local, it was constant. To my dad, it was nothing short of miraculous that Mom was actually home when she went into labor . . . exactly five minutes before Wanda. Since George was at work, Dad ended up driving both women to the hospital. They clutched each other in the backseat—two huge-bellied, panting, moaning women, both of them freaking out about the work they were missing. Dad sped all the way to the hospital, sure he'd get pulled over and arrested for being a suspected polygamist with a taste for overachievers.

Rayna and I were born exactly five hours apart—I'm the older one—and we've been inseparable ever since. We say we're twins with different parents.

The tabloids love to point out the difference in social status between Rayna and me, but to me, she's blood. My parents feel the same way. They've always made sure Rayna went to the same private schools I did, and she's been invited on every family vacation.

Still, to the rest of the world, she's not a Weston. I'm not sure that's such a bad deal. I *am* a Weston, and the main thing it's meant is a bunch of photographers chasing me from the minute I was born, writing about how I might affect Mom's career, or whether I'd follow in the Weston footsteps one day to change the world. My family name meant that two months into seventh grade, a photo spread appeared in *People* magazine: "Clea Raymond's Awkward Tween

Years!" It was filled with hideous pictures of me from camp the summer before—pictures I had no idea were even being snapped. There was one of me with sleep-knotted hair and thick glasses, another of me picking out a wedgie. There's nothing better for a twelve-year-old's blooming self-esteem than images like that papered all over her school. They gave me a stomachache that lasted until high school.

Rayna's an expert at glossing over bad moments like that. She always knew when my name was in magazines. She loved that I got to travel the world with my parents, and squealed with glee whenever I told her I went to some celebrity-laden event. She's never been jealous over any of it. And even though she's been around that stuff all her life, she never got jaded about it. She's always excited when she comes with me to a party, or an exclusive club, or an exotic vacation spot . . . or something like this winter break trip, where we got to do all three.

I didn't even realize I was dancing with my eyes closed until I felt a hand grip my arm and they snapped open.

"Clea!" Rayna shouted over the music, her eyes shiny from the drinks and the excitement of a new love of her life. *"Je vais aller chez Pierre!* He has a penthouse with a view of the Eiffel Tower. *C'est très bon, non?"*

Rayna clearly thought it was *très, très bon,* so I had to agree. *"Oui,"* I said, smiling. "Just be safe. You have his address?"

Rayna nodded, and I pulled out my phone so she could type it in.

"Pepper spray?" I asked.

Rayna rolled her eyes and pulled the cylinder from her purse. I nodded approvingly.

"Anything feels wrong, you call me. No matter what. And if you don't text me within twelve hours I'm calling the SWAT team."

"We're in France. There is no SWAT team," Rayna reminded me. Then she leaned close, touching our foreheads together and looking me straight in the eyes. "I will be fine. You will never lose me."

For the past year she'd been saying that almost every time we separated. Much as I appreciated the sentiment, I always winced at the "never." It seemed to be taunting fate. I'd told Rayna this, but she only laughed at my "crazy superstitions." Apparently it was fine to believe in fate delivering you a soulmate every night, but crazy to believe fate might chafe at being told what to do. I believed Rayna gave fate far too much credit for benevolence.

I stayed at the club only long enough so Rayna wouldn't see me leave. She'd feel bad if she thought I'd gone out only for her benefit. Back at the hotel, I dove greedily for the room safe and unlocked it to grab my camera.

For as long as I can remember, photography has been my escape. My father gave me my first camera when I was only four. "Remember, Clea," he told me, "taking pictures is a huge responsibility. Many cultures believe a photograph can capture one's soul."

As always, I'd listened solemnly to him, hanging on every word and believing it without question, even when Mom laughed and rolled her eyes. "Oh, Grant, look at her," she said, her voice filled with adoration for us both. "Her eyes are saucers. Tell her it's not true."

"It's not true," Dad agreed, but his back was to Mom and she couldn't see what I did: He was crossing his fingers. I grinned, thrilled to be Dad's co-conspirator.

From the minute Dad gave me the camera, I couldn't get enough of it. He loved that. He was also a photography buff, and he was proud that I could always hang for the long hours in his basement studio. Both he and Mom claim I was very mommy-oriented before I got into photography, but I don't remember that. In my memory, it was always Dad and me, talking, laughing, and sharing everything as we worked together to turn our pictures into art.

Rayna laughs at me. Given my antipathy for the paparazzi, she thinks it's hysterical that I'm so attached to my cameras. But to me, what I do is the anti-paparazzi. TMZsters want to capture surface. If a picture's in focus, it's great. My goal is to capture what the surface is hiding. There's a story behind every face, every landscape, every still life. There's a soul in every subject, and when my camera and I are really speaking, really working together properly, we can capture it.

In my hotel room, I placed the camera gently on my bed so I could pull on extra layers and brave the cold. I'd brought my favorite camera along for the trip—a DSLR my dad had bought me just before he left for his final GloboReach trip. Newer and supposedly better models have come out, but this one feels tailor-made for me. Quickly I yanked off the cocktail dress and heels and pulled on a pair of silk long johns, my favorite jeans, a turtleneck, a thick pullover sweater, a hoodie, and a knit beanie hat. No gloves—gloves form a barrier between me and the camera; they break our connection.

Bundled as much as I could, I pulled open the door to the balcony and stepped outside. The temperature had dipped below freezing, and ice rimmed the wrought-iron railings and furniture. I gave the skyline a cursory view, knowing I wouldn't *really* see it until I looked through the lens. I took a deep breath, savoring the moment, then lifted the camera to my eye. Immediately I started snapping. I could see it all from here: little cafés, markets and libraries tucked in until morning, and above it all, the breathtaking majesty of Notre Dame, glowing in spotlights that brought it vividly to life.

I stayed on the balcony for hours, capturing every tiny intricacy of the architecture, the street, the scattered people walking by. I snapped it all, and kept the Latin Quarter company until sunrise broke over the city and everything warmed just enough for me to realize my fingers had gone completely numb.

A perfect night; and I didn't have to sleep.

I walked back into the room, felt immediately blasted by the heat, and silently thanked myself for the foresight to turn up the thermostat before I started shooting.

My hands were too numb to dial the phone at all successfully, but after two failed attempts I managed. I asked room service for a hot cocoa, their largest pot of hot tea, and a chocolate croissant, making sure they'd leave it outside the door if I didn't answer. I planned to be in the shower until my skin turned lobster red and every bit of the cold was leached from my body.

Forty-five minutes later I was bundled in a cozy robe, sitting on my bed, drinking cocoa and munching the croissant. Heat still radiated from my body after the blisteringly wonderful shower, as delicious as the meal. Perfectly satisfied, I flipped on the news, curious if I might catch a glimpse of Mom. Where was she this week? I couldn't remember. Was it Israel? Moscow? Could she actually be here in Europe? I leaned back on a stack of pillows and settled in to watch . . .

. . . and the next thing I knew, I was surrounded by flames.

They were everywhere. I squeezed my eyes tight against the angry orange sear, but it didn't help. I knew it was there; even behind my eyes I could see it.

And the smell. The pungent odor of toxic chemicals melting out of plastics, rugs, electronics. The sick scent of burning hair. Human hair. My hair?

No. I saw him now. The man staggering around the inferno that had once been a hotel room, flames dancing over his arms, his legs, his hair. He pounded at the flames, but it only fueled them, and as they leaped down to his face, the man turned to me, and I saw my father's final agonized cry of—

"NO!" I gasped, bolting upright. My heart raced, and tears of despair rolled down my cheeks. Where was I? I clutched for my necklace and found only the thick folds of my robe. Frightened and shaken, I looked around, completely disoriented, my nose hunting for the smell of fire.

My eyes caught on the room service tray lying next to me on the bed. Chocolate croissant crumbs. Specific. Concrete. My ragged breathing smoothed, and I glanced out the window to find the comforting glow of Notre Dame. I focused on the cathedral, taking in longer and deeper breaths.

The therapist had told me the dreams would go away as time passed, but it had been a year since my dad disappeared, and they were still pretty constant. The therapist now claims it's because of the uncertainty. If I *knew* what happened, if there were any answers . . .

But there aren't. So my mind fills in the blanks with every horrible thing I've ever heard, read about, or seen. And since I've had the amazing opportunity to work as a photojournalist, I've seen all kinds of things.

In other words, my brain has a lot of great nightmare fodder.

I chastised myself over this last one, though. It was ridiculous. If I knew anything, I knew my father didn't die in a hotel fire. He hadn't been staying at a hotel; he'd been at a GloboReach outpost. So why would I dream about that?

My eyes drifted to the television, and it all made sense. There was a fire on the screen. I must have heard it in my sleep and incorporated it into my dream. I made a mental note not to watch the news when I fell asleep. The last thing I needed was help with my nightmares.

I winced, watching the fire. It was huge, devouring a large, beautiful apartment building that had to have been around since the 1800s. It made me sad to think something could have the fortitude to last over two hundred years, only to be destroyed in no time at all.

I turned the volume up, wanting to know more about the building and the people who were inside. My French was only okay, but it sounded like the fire had broken out somewhere on the upper floors of a building that was much coveted for its views of the Eiffel Tower.

My blood ran cold.

I had heard something about views of the Eiffel Tower tonight.

No . . . I was jumping to conclusions . . . there was no way . . .

I heard Rayna's voice in my head. *Je vais aller chez Pierre! He has a penthouse with a view of the Eiffel Tower. C'est très bon, non?*

Still, there were a lot of apartments in Paris with views of the Eiffel Tower. The chances that this building was the same one . . .

I grabbed my phone and scrolled to where Rayna had written Pierre's address, then glared at the TV anchors.

"Come on, come on," I urged them. "Tell me where it is! What's the address?"

"Le feu est a vingt-quatre rue des Soeurs," the female anchor finally said.

The world stopped.

The addresses were the same.

"No!" I cried out. "Please, no. No, no, no . . ."

I pounded out Rayna's number and waited forever for the phone to ring. "Pick up, Rayna, *please* pick up."

Nothing. No answer.

"Shit!" I hung up, yanked on my clothes, and raced out of the room, doubling back for only a second to grab my camera. It was sheer instinct. Whatever panic I was feeling about Rayna, the fire was a news story, and I take pictures of news stories.

"J'ai besoin d'un taxi maintenant!" I snapped to the doorman as I ran outside, then followed it up with a perfunctory, *"S'il vous plaît."* But the doorman had heard the desperation in my voice and had already darted into the street to flag one down.

This was taking far too long. Could I run the two miles faster? No, better to wait, but standing there was making me insane. I had to do something. I checked my watch: nine a.m. Three a.m. in New London, Connecticut. It didn't matter. I called his number.

He answered on the third ring, sounding completely awake and alert, though I knew he had been asleep for hours.

"Clea? Are you okay?"

Thank God for caller ID. Ben knew I wouldn't call in the middle of the night unless it was absolutely vital.

"Ben! Ben, it's about Rayna. There's a fire—a huge fire!"

My voice broke, and I started to sob. I couldn't keep it together, not if something happened to Rayna. I couldn't.

"Take a deep breath and tell me. Tell me everything." Ben's voice was calm and steady now. I loved that about him; the more difficult and emotional a situation, the more he'd step back and handle it logically and methodically. His voice had been my security blanket a lot this past year.

"I don't know," I said. The doorman had finally found a cab and I raced inside, shouting Pierre's address to the driver. *"Vite, s'il vous plaît—vite!"* I curled into the backseat of the car, hugging myself as I told Ben what I'd seen.

"Okay." Ben's voice soothed me from nearly four thousand miles away. "Don't panic. You don't know anything yet. You're going there now, right?"

"As fast as I can," I said, reaching into my purse and pulling out a handful of euros, which I held out to the driver. *"Plus vite, s'il vous plaît,"* I urged.

"Great," Ben said. "Just talk to me until you get there."

I have no idea what I would do without Ben. My circle of trusted friends comes to exactly two: Ben and Rayna. Not even enough to make a circle—a line segment of trusted friends.

I spoke to Ben every second of the ten-minute ride. I had to. The sound of my own voice reaching out to him was the only thing that kept my entire body from flying apart and scattering into molecules of panic.

"Arrêtez! Arrêtez!!!" I shouted to the cab driver. Not that it was necessary; road blockades prevented us from going any farther. "I'm here!" I told Ben. "I'm getting out; I'll call you back the minute I know anything."

"I'll wait," Ben said, and I knew he would.

I shoved another handful of euros at the taxi driver, then ran out and immediately shut my eyes against the acrid air. I yanked my turtleneck collar over my nose and mouth to filter the smoke and ash as I ran the last block to the blazing building, pushing through gawkers at every step. Fire trucks were on the scene, but the water from their hoses seemed like an insignificant trickle, a child's water pistol in the face of an inferno.

"RAYNA!" I screamed up to the wall of flames. "RAYNA!!!!"

"Clea!"

I spun around wildly, needing to see her face like I needed air, needing to make sure she was okay, that she wasn't calling to me from a stretcher, gasping out her last—

"Clea . . . Clea, it's okay. I'm okay . . . I'm right here."

There she was, bundled into sweats and a long wool coat five sizes too large for her, her curls hidden by a massive gray hat with earflaps—a look that could have been pulled off effectively only by someone in 1930s Siberia . . . or a supremely angular male model.

"Oh my God, Rayna!" I cried, pulling her into my arms and squeezing too hard. I couldn't help it. I needed proof that she was really there.

"I'm fine. Pierre and I went out for coffee. We weren't even here when the fire started." She pulled back just enough to press her forehead into mine and look into my eyes. "I told you you'll never lose me, remember?"

"Don't," I warned, but the panic had already drained enough that I could smile. I hugged her again, and even when we pulled away we kept our arms wrapped around each other.

"Have you ever seen anything like it?" she asked solemnly, and I followed her gaze to the apartment building, its entire midsection now engulfed in leaping flames.

I *had* seen things like it, but that didn't lessen the impact. Fire is magnetic—an almost illicit combination of destructive force and awe-inspiring beauty. With an effort, I turned away from the dancing slashes of flame to the scene on the street. I saw the grim determination of the firefighters, their faces betraying no emotion. I saw the onlookers, split between the curious and the personally affected—the former gaping upward in a state of exalted wonder, the latter huddled together in frightened groups, or chain-smoking and pacing like Pierre. I saw the dissonance of rainbows as the sun glinted off the water from the fire hoses.

"Itchy trigger finger?" Rayna asked, smiling. I followed her gaze to my right hand, which had already removed my camera from its bag. "You should," she said. "I'm going to check on Pierre. And if you give me your phone, I'll call Ben back and let him know everything's okay. Assuming you called him," she added with a grin.

Rayna knew me far too well. I gave her one last squeeze, then handed her the phone and disappeared behind my camera, blending seamlessly into the scene. It was where I belonged. It felt right.

I had absolutely no idea I was taking pictures that would change my life forever.

two

BACK HOME in Connecticut, I stared at my computer, poring over the image on the screen. My eyes burned from lack of sleep and four hours in front of the monitor. After a long plane ride, an endless wait at the baggage carousel, and a traffic-filled slog up the highway, Rayna and I had arrived home in Niantic early in the afternoon Eastern time, but well into the evening Paris time. Exhausted, Rayna and I hugged each other good-bye and split off into our separate houses to crash.

Except I couldn't. I had a sixteen-gig compact

flash card filled with trip pictures screaming for my attention.

I loaded them onto my hard drive and started sorting. It would take me ages to really do justice to every shot I'd snapped over the three-week trip, so I let my instincts winnow them down. I allowed myself the briefest scan of each image, saving the ones that grabbed me to a special file. Again and again I went through the process, giving myself a little more time on each picture with every round, pulling aside the ones my eyes couldn't stop drifting to, the ones that struck me in a place of pure instinct and emotion.

It took hours, but eventually I narrowed them down to twenty pictures, spanning all portions of our trip: Trafalgar Square at night; a snarling gargoyle leaping off a column at Prague's St. Vitus's Cathedral; Rayna with her back to the Trevi Fountain, following tradition by tossing a coin with her right hand over her left shoulder.

But my eyes kept going back to a picture of the fire at Pierre's apartment building. I clicked it so it took up the whole screen. It was a shot of two firefighters on the ground. The smoke had grown thick by this point, and both wore oxygen tanks on their backs and cone-shaped masks that obscured their entire faces. Their thick black suits, yellow gloves, and yellow helmets covered them entirely, yet their emotion was crystal clear. They leaned back in perfect synch, holding the thick green hose between them, shooting water up at the flames, the very angle of their bodies and faces signaling grit, determination, and hope.

The image was gripping and kinetic, yet as I ran my eyes over it again and again I wasn't drawn to the firefighters, but to the fire truck far behind them.

I enlarged the picture, zoomed in on the truck. There was an indentation along its side panel, the place where the hoses connected and the water valves turned on and off. The image was shadowed by something, but it was still too small and I couldn't see it clearly.

I enlarged the picture again, centering that one spot on the side panel. Now I understood; the shadow was from a man. He looked young, in his early twenties maybe, though it was hard to make out his features, since he wasn't looking at the lens. He faced sideways, one hand gripping the ladder embedded in the panel wall. His head was downcast, and every muscle in his body seemed to coil with clenched tension.

Could he be a firefighter? He was built like one, but he wasn't in uniform. He wore a black leather jacket over jeans and a gray T-shirt. And though he had the facial scruff of someone who'd been on the job all night, he wasn't engaged with the fire at all. He seemed wrapped in his own thoughts. His mane of dark, tousled hair, chiseled cheekbones, and thick eyebrows were stunning, but some inward pain twisted his eyes and mouth away from beauty and toward something more difficult and profound.

I couldn't take my eyes off him.

I wondered what was going on in his head. Had the fire started in his apartment? I imagined him on the scene as the engines arrived, screaming at the flames as if sheer will could stop them. Or perhaps he was still inside when the firefighters came, raging against the growing inferno, coughing from the smoke as he defiantly pounded out licks of flame with blankets wet from his sink. I could see him struggling against the firefighters as they pulled him out of his apartment. I could imagine—

The sound of the doorbell brought me back to reality.

"Piri?" I called, then remembered our housekeeper wasn't here today. I'd given her the day off so I could decompress on my own. Reluctantly I left my computer and went down to the front door. No one was there, but a large bouquet of irises, with blooms in all the colors of the rainbow, had been left on the stoop. They were beautiful. I carried them inside and placed them on the kitchen table, then opened the card.

Welcome home! Sorry I couldn't be there. I love you and I'll see you next week when I get back from Israel. Love, Mom.

That was it. Despite her choice of blooms, she didn't mention Dad at all. She hadn't since the day after he was buried: in a casket with no body, under a headstone that would never mark his final resting place. She had told me flat out that she couldn't handle speaking about him, so we wouldn't. Period. It was hard at first, but after she won her Senate seat and became a prominent member of the Foreign Relations Committee, constantly traveling around the world, we had so little time together that I didn't want to ruin it with anything that would upset her. So I hold my tongue and keep our conversations light. It keeps a chasm between us, but since there's no way for me to bridge it without breaking her, I let it go.

But she had sent irises, my dad's favorite flower. I touched the charm around my neck and felt happy and empty at the same time. I wanted to call my mom and tell her I understood what she couldn't say. I wanted to pour out my heart about my nightmares and how broken I still felt inside, but I knew she'd find an excuse to get off the phone the minute I started.

I couldn't find comfort with Mom . . . but maybe I could with Dad. It wasn't ideal, but it always seemed to help a little. I plucked one of the irises from the vase and walked upstairs to Dad's office.

Most people would think Grant Raymond, as the most renowned heart surgeon in the world, would take pride in keeping things clean. Pristine, perhaps. Even sterile. Those people would be wrong. My dad wasn't sloppy or dirty, but he liked his surroundings to reflect his thinking: multibranched, creative, and divergent. In the operating room he needed absolute order; everywhere else he thrived on absolute chaos.

Another quirk of Dad's was that although he could remember an infinite number of intricate surgical maneuvers and enough random details and trivia to run any *Jeopardy!* champion under the table, he found it patently impossible to remember basic things like phone numbers, appointments, or what in the world he had actually walked into the room to do. To mitigate this flaw, he wrote everything down, usually on whatever was handiest. This left his office looking like the heavens had opened and rained leaves of paper for forty days and forty nights. Popping up from this churning ocean were models of the human heart, reference books, and notebooks full of inspired scrawls.

Illustrious hospitals and medical journals from all over the world had begged to send experts to sift through everything, just in case Dad had left notes that might lead to major leaps forward in cardio health. Mom paid no attention to these requests, but someone had to deal with them. That left me. I saw the experts' argument. I even knew logically that they were right—the world deserved to benefit from Dad's knowledge. If something in his office could save or improve a single life, Dad would want that information available. But strangers going through this room seemed like the ultimate degradation. Like an autopsy. I knew it made no sense, but it was how I felt. Maybe in a few years I'd change my mind. Or maybe never.

I picked my way to Dad's desk and sat down in his chair. Mimicking his favorite pose, I leaned all the way back, surveyed the glorious chaos, and waited for that feeling of his presence to settle in like it always did.

But it didn't.

Something was wrong.

Something in the room was different.

I couldn't place it exactly, but I could feel it. Things had been moved, or altered somehow. Placed back afterward, maybe, so it wouldn't be so obvious, but there was an ineffable change in the room. I felt the edge of panic hit—this office was the closest thing I had to my dad. Changing anything in here changed *him*, or what was left of him for me.

Was it Piri? Had she tried to clean in here? Impossible. Piri revered Dad. Despite her overwhelming belief in the cleanliness/godliness connection, she would defend to the death his right to make any choice . . . even one she found personally heartbreaking. The few times Dad had left the door open and Piri saw inside, she held her breath and crossed herself for protection, but she walked right by.

But if it wasn't Piri, then who? Who else had access to the house while I was away? Mom? She would never step inside here. Ben had keys. He loved my dad. He might have come inside to see him, like I do, but he would never move anything. He wouldn't do that to me. Same with Rayna's family.

Could it be someone without keys? Someone who'd broken in while I was gone? Someone who waited for Piri to leave at the end of the day, then slipped inside and snooped through my dad's things, opening drawers, moving things, changing them around . . .

"Stop!" I said it out loud. I was being ridiculous and jumping to conclusions. I'd done that a lot this past year. "Extreme Thinking," my therapist called it. Not uncommon in people who have been through an unexpected tragedy. When it happened, I was supposed to step back and look at things as rationally as possible.

So, rationally then . . . what specifically was different in here? I didn't know. Maybe nothing . . . except I still felt the cold sense that something was wrong.

I rose, shaking my head. This was crazy. I had to let it go. Yet even as I left the office, I couldn't help staring and trying to pinpoint what had changed. . . .

Then a low voice murmured in my ear. "Clea."

I screamed and shot an immediate hammer punch to the side.

"Whoa!" cried Ben. He reeled back to avoid my fist and tripped over the rug, tumbling to the ground and spilling a fresh mug of coffee over his gray shawl-neck sweater.

"OH!" he gasped. "Hot. Very, very hot. Oh, not good."

"Ben! Oh my God, wait—" I darted into the bathroom and grabbed a hand towel, then raced back to him, knelt down, and sopped the spilled coffee from his chest. "I'm so sorry. I didn't know you were there! You didn't say anything!"

"I yelled from downstairs . . . I thought you'd heard me."

A strange smell tickled my nose, and I bent closer to Ben, just inches from his face. "What's that smell?" I asked.

"Cardamom clove coffee," he said, gesturing to the now empty mug on the floor beside us. "I thought you might like it."

"I like the smell. Maybe you should wear it as a cologne."

"Could work," he agreed. "You could give a testimonial that it makes women crazy."

"Not crazy—nimble. Ten years of Krav Maga gives you catlike reflexes. If you'd been an intruder . . ."

The idea brought back all my questions and I quickly got up and led Ben to my dad's office. "Do you see anything different in there?"

Ben looked, then shook his head. "It looks the same to me. Did you change anything?"

"No! I wouldn't!" I retorted. "Someone did, though, I think. It feels different in there. Tampered with."

Ben nodded, hands in his pockets—his thoughtful mode. "Okay," he said, "what is it that feels different? Has anything moved? Is something missing?"

"I can't tell," I admitted. "It's not like I see anything specific. It's just a feeling."

"I get that," Ben said. "I trust your feelings. Just . . . maybe some of it comes from being away for so long. Three weeks. It's your longest trip since . . ."

His voice trailed off, but I knew what he meant. It was my longest trip since the funeral. It was true. It was also true that I'd been up since six in the morning Paris time, and it was now six in the evening in Connecticut: midnight Paris time. And of course there was my propensity for Extreme Thinking.

"You're right," I said. "And I'm exhausted. Maybe I should take a nap." Though even as I said it, I thought about the pictures waiting on my computer screen and knew they'd be far more likely than sleep to get my attention.

"Actual likelihood of that?" Like Rayna, Ben knew how to read my mind. I smiled at him.

"I missed you," I said.

"Missed you, too. Welcome home."

We moved in to hug each other, then I sprang back seconds before getting smushed against his still-sopping-wet sweater.

"Ben!"

"Ooh, poor form on my part," he said, and peeled off his sodden sweater. He wore a thin white T-shirt underneath. The coffee spill had left the shirt a bit damp, and it clung slightly to his chest in a way that made me stare and caught my voice in my throat.

That was ridiculous, of course. Ben and I had the kind of friendship where we talked about things like that. I could tease him about his suddenly well-toned body; he'd make some kind of self-effacing joke and parry by bringing up something absurd he'd seen about me in a magazine . . .

But I didn't say a word. And I didn't stop looking. Clearly I was in a sleep-deprived haze.

"You could still try the coffee," he offered. "There's plenty in the sweater. I can just wring it right into the mug."

I shook off my reverie. "Tempting offer, but no thanks. You really need to give up on the coffee thing. I'm never converting from tea."

"We'll see," he said. He set the wet sweater on the hand towel, then turned to me with his arms out. "Better?"

"Much," I said, and closed the distance between us so he could fold me into his arms.

"Hel-*lo! Pleeeeeease* tell me I'm interrupting something!" It was Rayna, and at the sound of her voice, Ben and I sheepishly pulled apart. Again, ridiculous. Hugging was nothing unusual for us. Granted, Ben was usually wearing more than a thin T-shirt at the time. . . .

"Why is it I'm hearing no one when they come into the house?" I asked.

"Big house," Rayna said. "Come on—my mom's throwing us a welcome home party at our place."

"Tonight?" I asked.

"Immediately. Unless I can tell my mom there are . . . extenuating circumstances."

She said the last part with a leer that lingered on Ben's chest and made him blush. Rayna's entire family had spent the last two years dying for Ben and me to get together. They seemed to be under the impression that my parents hired him to be my boyfriend, not my international adviser.

It's hard to believe that I've known Ben for only two years, and even more bizarre that at first I wanted nothing to do with him. Mom and Dad hired Ben without my knowledge soon after I started getting photojournalism assignments around the world, including some less-than-savory locations. I was furious, imagining a brainless meathead of a bodyguard who'd hang like an albatross around my neck.

I should have given my parents more credit. Their main worry wasn't that I'd be physically harmed. We'd had a lot of long talks, and they trusted me to avoid any obvious danger. They also reserved the right to veto any assignments they didn't think were appropriate until I turned eighteen. So my parents didn't hire Ben for his brawn, they hired him for his brains. At twenty, he already has a doctorate, speaks more languages than should be humanly possible, and knows something about pretty much everything, though his specialties are world history and mythology. His knowledge keeps me safer when I travel than any ham-fisted tough guy.

But to Rayna and Wanda (and probably George, too, since he always follows the women in his life), Ben is my *soulmate*.

"No extenuating circumstances," Ben said. "Sweater malfunction. Let's go to the party."

Fifteen minutes later we were all at Rayna's house, where Wanda had created an all-American feast. Her dining room table groaned under red, white, and blue plates of hot dogs *and* pigs-in-blankets, hamburgers, fried chicken, mashed potatoes, biscuits, and of course apple pie à la mode for dessert. It was an insane amount of food for just the five of us, and we ate until we nearly burst. Then afterward Ben reigned supreme in a marathon game of charades. I didn't get back home until midnight: six a.m. Paris time. I had been up for twenty-four hours. My eyes burned with fatigue, and every muscle in my body screamed for rest.

I nearly made it. I'd washed up and was about to stagger into bed . . . when I let my eyes drift to my computer. My screensaver flashed a slide show of my favorite pictures, but all I could think about was the tortured man from the fire and the other nineteen images I'd chosen so many hours earlier.

I sat at my desk and pressed a button to clear the screensaver. I stared a moment at the man in the fire truck again, so fascinating in his torment. I wanted to print out his image and add it to my portfolio, but I'd had to enlarge the picture so much just to see him, I'd never be able to get more than a granulated print.

I reduced the picture to the bottom of my screen and scanned the other nineteen images, waiting to see which would demand my attention first. I clicked on a picture of Rayna in front of the Parthenon in Athens. She was in a flowing white dress, her arms raised in a goddesslike pose as her long red curls blew behind her. The setting sun lit her whole body aglow, and the effect was absolutely magnificent . . . except for a small knot of tourists I couldn't frame out of the shot.

Time to start cropping.

I reframed the image, but as I did I noticed something strange in the crowd of tourists. A familiar cheekbone and a hard-set jaw.

No. It was impossible.

Instead of cropping out the tourists, I enlarged

them to twice, three times their size. They were six members of a single group, all in matching powder blue T-shirts that read IT'S GREEK TO ME TOURS. Every one of them stared at the monument, pointing or taking pictures.

Then there was the seventh person, who stared directly at the camera. He was obscured by three of the powder blue shirt crew, so I could only see half his face: a sweep of hair, one carved cheekbone, one piercing brown eye . . . but there was no doubt it was him.

My heart started thumping as I moved the Parthenon photo to one side of the screen and pulled up the Paris photo next to it, both enlarged to focus on one man. It was the *same* man; the man whom I now realized had been with Rayna and me not only in Paris at the end of our trip, but also in Greece three weeks before.

Panic welled up in me. How had I not noticed him? Ever since the summer camp photo incident, I'd prided myself on being constantly alert, aware, and vigilant about just this kind of thing, and yet I'd had no idea this man was stalking us through Europe. And he *was* stalking us. Why else would he be at both ends of our trip? It couldn't be coincidence. That wasn't possible . . . was it?

I stared again at both images. The lone civilian among the firemen, the outsider amid the tour group . . . this man was completely out of place in both pictures. Alone, either could easily be explained away, but together they pointed to something more sinister.

My eyes ran over the other thumbnails I'd pulled aside, and I felt a chill race over my body. If this stalker had been with us at both the beginning and end of our trip . . . was it possible he was with us the whole time? The very idea made my skin crawl, but didn't it make sense? And what if these pictures had reached out to me not because of their artistry, but because I'd sensed the danger I'd somehow missed in real life?

Any exhaustion I'd felt was now gone. My skin prickled with fear as I reduced both images on my screen and pulled up another thumbnail. This one was the Sacré-Coeur Basilica in Montmartre. I enlarged it and scanned for that face. I didn't see it, but I hadn't seen it right away in the other pictures either. I enlarged again and kept scanning, my knuckles white as I gripped the mouse.

There.

A shadow on one of the highest parapets.

I zoomed in closer, and my forehead broke out in sweat.

He was there. His back was turned, but I saw the hair, the leather jacket, the jeans, the muscular build . . . it was him, and he stood in a spot I knew was absolutely off-limits to tourists.

So how did he get there? And why?

My first thought was actually comforting. He could be a government bodyguard Rayna and I weren't supposed to have noticed. That had happened before—Mom had made people upset enough that they'd threatened our family, and there had been times when she'd put a tail on me, but kept it a secret so I wouldn't get scared. If that's what this man was, it would certainly explain his access to the parapet. It was still weird that I hadn't seen him, since I'd always pegged the "secret" bodyguards before, but maybe he was just better at his job than the others.

Or maybe he'd been more careful than the others because he *wasn't* there to guard me. Maybe instead of protecting me from a threat . . . he *was* the threat.

I quickly enlarged the other thumbnails, one at a time. I ran my eyes over the backgrounds, the corners, the most seemingly inconsequential parts of each photo, enlarging and enlarging until every time . . . I saw him. He was always there. Though the pictures were all from different parts of our trip, different parts of Europe, he was there. Always obscured, in the background, so small you would never notice him unless you were specifically looking, but *always there*.

I was shaking now, positive this man had wanted to harm me and possibly Rayna (kidnap us? kill us?) during our trip, and it was only by chance that he hadn't found the perfect opportunity to do it. I was about to make an emergency call to my mother when I opened the final thumbnail: a gargoyle high on the walls of Prague's St. Vitus's Cathedral. I had taken the shot with a zoom lens: just the gargoyle leaping off the balcony, with only a window and the cathedral's facade behind it.

I zoomed in on the window, assuming I'd find the man peering out of it.

He wasn't there, which meant he couldn't possibly be in the shot. There was nowhere else for a person to hide.

Still, I couldn't help but search the enlarged photo, studying it edge to edge.

I finally found a shadow high in the corner of

the frame, and fresh goose bumps danced up my arms.

I didn't want to enlarge it. I didn't want to look any closer . . . but I had to.

I zoomed in on the image one more time and focused on the shadow.

It was him.

He stood with his hands in the pockets of his leather jacket. He lounged back on the wall of the cathedral, gazing thoughtfully off into the distance without a bit of tension in his body. Like he was waiting for a bus.

Except he was over a hundred feet in the air, and he stood on nothing.

Nothing.

The mouse rattled in my shaking hand and I let it go, but I couldn't stop staring at the picture. Who was this man? *What* was he? Ideas bolted through my brain, but every one of them was impossible.

But so was standing in midair.

In a flash of wild inspiration, I grabbed my camera and snapped ten pictures, spinning around in my chair to get the bookcase, the closet, the bed . . . every section of the room. I frantically uploaded them onto the computer and started poring over them one at a time, enlarging them and straining my eyes to find any unusual shadow, any half-blurred image.

There was nothing.

My heart slowed as I kept scanning. Despite my crazy thoughts, it seemed like the man really was just a flesh-and-blood stalker. I was actually relieved.

Then I opened up the tenth photo and screamed out loud.

It was my darkened closet . . . with the man inside the door.

three

I STARED AT THE SCREEN, FROZEN.

Inwardly I chastised myself. I had *expected* to see him, right? It was what I imagined might happen. It was why I took the pictures of my room in the first place.

But imagining it and seeing it were two very different things. The theory I could chalk up to lack of sleep, but this . . .

I still hadn't turned away from the computer screen to look at the closet. I couldn't. I was fairly certain he wasn't really there, but I couldn't shake the idea that he *was*. And I knew that if I turned and saw him, I'd come completely unhinged.

I heard footsteps and felt the rush of air as a hand reached out, grabbing at my throat. . . .

I screamed and wheeled to my right. There was nothing there.

But I could see the closet now. It was right in front of me, door ajar, same way it was two minutes ago when I'd taken its picture.

Still, I had to know for sure. My heart thudding in my ears, I walked to the closet door, reached for the knob, and flung it all the way open, half expecting the man to leap out at me.

But of course he didn't. The closet was empty.

Which brought me back to the impossible: that the man with the clenched jaw hadn't been in *any* of those places with Rayna and me . . . but had still appeared in my pictures.

But *how*?

I ripped the camera from my computer and clicked off the monitor. I needed to sleep. This would all make more sense after I slept. I staggered into my bed, pretending that it was perfectly normal for me to flick on every single light first. But when I lay down under the full blaze of every lamp in the room, my comforter wrapped tightly around me like a protective cocoon, I couldn't do it. Every time I closed my eyes, the man's face burned in my mind, and my eyes snapped open again.

Giving in to the sleepless night, I snaked my hand out of the covers to grab the remote, and searched for something innocuous.

The Food Network. Perfect.

I turned the volume all the way up to drown out my thoughts, propped myself up with a sea of pillows, and let myself zone out into a trancelike oblivion.

Somehow I fell asleep, but for the first time in ages, my dreams weren't tortured. Quite the opposite.

I stood by the piano in a small, crowded speakeasy, my fringed dress and iris-charm necklace shimmying along with me as I belted out an impossibly high final note. The room burst into whistles and applause when I finished, and I ate it up.

"Delia Rivers!" Eddie hollered proudly around the cigar in his mouth. His suit strained over his gut as he rose to put his arm around my shoulders.

Eddie owned the speakeasy. He owned most of Chicago, actually. He certainly owned me. He wasn't the kind of guy you wanted to cross—not if you valued your life. But even as he planted a sloppy kiss on my cheek, I couldn't resist glancing at the piano player. He bent low over his keyboard, but he peered up to meet my eyes and gave me a bittersweet smile that reached out and grabbed me by the heart.

Just then Eddie's boy Richie burst in. "Boss!" he cried, but before he could finish, he caught the look between the piano player and me. Richie raised his eyebrows at me imploringly. He didn't want me to get in trouble. He was a good friend, and he was right, but I was too far gone for that to matter.

"What is it?" Eddie roared.

"Sorry, Boss," Richie said. "It's a raid!"

Immediately the whole mess of us poured out the back of the speakeasy. We weren't in any real danger: Eddie owned the cops, too. But part of the deal was we made it look good by skipping out at raid time. Only Eddie and his core crew stayed to make the place look like the respectable, alcohol-free establishment it was supposed to be.

Freedom. A whole hour, at least. I clicked down the streets until I knew I was alone, then made a beeline for the alley behind the closed-down theater. My piano player was already there, and the knots in my stomach grew and then disappeared as I ran the rest of the way and launched myself into his arms, kissing him like my life depended on it.

"It kills me to see you with him, Delia," he said, pulling away just enough to pierce me with his soulful eyes. "Run away with me. We'll go to Hollywood. You've always wanted to get into movies."

I blushed and looked away. "Everyone wants to get into movies."

"You're not everyone. You're talented. But it's more than that. People can't take their eyes off you when you perform."

"I perform in a bar the size of a closet. There's nowhere else to look."

He gently lifted my chin so our eyes met. "I wish you could see yourself the way I see you. You have no idea how special you are. You can have everything you ever dreamed of. We both can."

His words gave me goose bumps, and for a second I believed it. I could even see it: the two of us running off, getting a little place together, singing and playing in little dives while we worked our way toward that big break . . .

But I didn't have that kind of charmed life. There was only one path for me.

"I could never leave," I said. "Eddie'd kill me if I did."

"You don't think I'd protect you? I'd die for you, Olivia."

It was a slap, and I backed away. "Olivia?"

"Delia," he backpedaled. He reached for me, but I shook away.

"It's not the first time that's happened. What is she, your wife?"

A shadow crossed the angles of his face before he answered. "No, she's not. I told you, what happened with her . . . it was just . . ." His thick eyebrows furrowed as he tried to find the words, but he couldn't. "It was a long time ago. I'm so sorry, Delia. Please . . . just look at me."

I knew I'd be done for if I did, but I couldn't help it. His eyes drew me in, and what I saw there was raw and scarred . . . but it didn't lie. He was telling the truth, and the truth was more awful than he could say.

"I don't know what she did to you." I sighed, letting him fold me back into his arms. "But if I ever see that girl, I'll kill her."

He didn't answer. He just gave me that melancholy smile, then placed his hand on my cheek and looked at me like he was memorizing my face. I got chills as he leaned in close and kissed me. . . .

I sat up, dazed and disoriented. The television screamed turkey-basting directions at me, and reality settled in: my room. My bed. The Food Network.

I grabbed the remote and turned off the TV. It had all been just a dream, but it felt so real. And the guy, the piano player . . . it was the man from my pictures. I could still feel his lips on mine as if I actually knew their touch, and part of me longed to close my eyes and slip back into the fantasy, but the sun streaming through my window wouldn't let me fall back to sleep.

Instead I padded to my computer and turned on the monitor. There he was, staring right at me. It was the same image that had terrified me last night, but I felt none of that now. I enlarged the picture, zooming in on his eyes.

"I wish you could see yourself the way I see you," he had said in my dream, and I looked deeper and deeper into those dark, magnetic pools as if I really could see myself there, just as he imagined me. . . .

Until I burst out laughing. What was wrong

with me? Suddenly I had become Rayna: One vivid dream and I was living a fantasy.

Reality check: Dreams were the brain's way of sorting out things left unsettled in our waking lives. A phantom stalker was about as unsettling as it could get, so my brain cast him as my star-crossed lover in the middle of the Roaring Twenties to make him less scary. And it worked—I wasn't afraid of him anymore, which meant I could start approaching the pictures logically.

For starters, I had to take anything paranormal off the table. That was the one area where I was more like my mom. Dad may have been a scientist, but he loved to contemplate things "beyond human understanding." He funded some of the world's most ridiculous wild-goose chases, and would rave about the game-changing potential of a real life Fountain of Youth, or Healing Caves, or undiscovered ancient creatures that still lived and could unlock the secret to long-term survival.

Through these projects, Dad was actually responsible for some interesting archaeological finds, but when the New Age fanboys choked the Internet with chatter about their cosmic, transcendental significance, Mom and I had to tune out. We knew the truth: There was no such thing as "beyond human understanding." With enough information, anything could be explained. The images on my camera may have seemed impossible, but that was only because I didn't have the right information to comprehend them . . . yet.

My heart jumped as I heard clanking and clanging downstairs, but I quickly relaxed. It was Piri. For years she had been like a crazy Hungarian grandmother, doting on me with equal parts rich traditional desserts (strudels and tortes), and rich traditional superstitions (always sit when you visit a baby, or you'll take away its dreams). Mom and I rolled our eyes at those, but Dad of course ate them up, writing them down and cataloging them in his studio with all his other research on ancient and modern mythologies.

Since Dad's death, I'd tried not to spend a lot of time around Piri. It sounds absurd to say, but she seemed to be taking it harder than any of us. Her head bowed whenever she touched anything of his, her eyes welled up with tears, and the house reverberated with her heavy sighs. It made me angry sometimes, the way she was allowed to indulge in mourning when the rest of us had to move on. Most of the time I ignored it, though. I just kept busy and out of her way.

Her arrival now was a great excuse to get out of the house. I also needed a break to clear my mind. Plus I was hungry. I peeked at my watch and saw it was well after noon. No wonder I was hungry—I'd slept longer than I had in ages.

I picked up the phone and called Ben. "Dalt's in sixty?" I asked.

"Done," he said. "You want to bring the board?"

"Depends . . . you okay with humiliation?"

"Bring the board."

"See you soon."

I hung up and ran to the shower. Thirty minutes later I was out the door, cribbage board in hand.

"Bye, Piri!" I shouted. I was already in my car and pulling away when I saw Piri appear on the threshold, tossing a small cup of water out after me, "so luck would flow like water in my direction."

Madness.

I turned up the radio and sang loud and off-key as I hit the highway, relishing the ride. Mom had offered to buy me a new car for my last birthday, but I wouldn't give up my much-loved and battle-scarred Ford Bronco with the funky mint green paint job until it fell apart on me. I'd bought it myself, saving up my earnings until I could afford the ancient beauty. Every shiny rental I drove when I traveled reminded me how much I adored my own car. We knew each other, we worked well together. . . . Why would I mess with that?

I saw Ben in the window the minute I pulled into the parking lot. Dalt's Diner—a twenty-four-hour greasy-spoon pit stop for truckers cruising I-95, or for nearby Connecticut College students desperate for a three a.m. meal—had been around forever. Ben discovered it because the college employed him part-time as an adjunct professor. He gave a couple of lectures a semester, and lived on campus in faculty housing, so he knew all the student haunts.

Dalt's resembled a train car: one long row of booths pushed against the outside windows, plus a counter by the grill on which they managed to make nearly everything on the menu. I'm fairly certain even the spaghetti was tossed onto the grill before it was served. Dalt's was pretty much the best restaurant ever.

I yanked on my sunglasses and baseball cap before I left my car. College students loved to approach me and talk politics, medicine, or New Age insanity as if I could actually channel one of my parents for them. It was great that they were so interested, but I wasn't my parents, and I could never handle the conversations to their satisfaction, so they always walked away disappointed.

"Eager for defeat?" I asked, noting the paper and cards Ben had already set on the table.

"Fascinating comment," he said as he flipped through the yellow legal pad, "seeing as at last check, you owe me seventy-five cents."

"A temporary blip," I conceded, slipping into the bench across from him and setting the cribbage board on the table.

Ben grew up in a family that adored cribbage. I knew nothing about the game when we met, but I felt bad that the computer was his only challenger, so I asked him to teach me. Not surprisingly, Ben's an excellent teacher, and within a few weeks we were pretty evenly matched. I knew I had arrived in the cribbage world when he proudly presented me with my own board. I was thrilled, and attached a length of braided rope to one end so I could hang the board from a hook in my room—a place of honor.

That's when we began our ritual marathon games for money—a quarter a game. Twice a year we paid up: once on my birthday, once on his. The most either of us ever had to pay was a dollar, but it wasn't about the money, it was about bragging rights. It was also about tradition: We always used my board, and Ben's cards and yellow legal pad. It was sheer blasphemy to even consider changing any of those elements.

But cribbage was for afterward. "What's going on with Alissa?" I asked.

"Alissa is a very popular woman," Ben said, pulling a leather notebook binder from his canvas satchel.

I laughed. Alissa was me.

It was Rayna's idea. Since I was a kid, I'd loved the idea of being a photojournalist. I always put aside my best pictures for my "portfolio," which I hid under my bed. Only Rayna knew my plan; that way no one would ask me about it, and I wouldn't have to tell anyone if I failed. I waited until I was sixteen, then sent my portfolio everyplace I admired: magazines, newspapers, e-zines, TV news . . . everywhere. I spent the next weeks so anxious I could barely put a sentence together. I'd agonized over every picture in the portfolio, and I thought it was really strong.

Finally the responses poured in . . . every single one a rejection. A hundred different versions of

Thanks, but this is a serious publication. We don't hire celebrity children for vanity projects.

I was completely mortified. I buried the portfolio in the attic and swore I'd never show anyone my pictures again.

Rayna didn't give up so easily. She exhumed the portfolio and sent it out under the pseudonym "Alissa Grande." She later told me that the name was her inside joke: Alissa means "truth," Grande "large," so while the name was a lie, it was in support of a "greater truth": an honest opinion of my skills.

A week after she sent out the portfolios, I received my first assignment, and they haven't stopped coming since. It's not like I make a ton of money or anything, but I get to take pictures that matter, and share them with the world, which I love.

While I was in Europe with Rayna, Ben had manned Alissa Grande's e-mail, voice mail, and P.O. box for me.

"Did I miss anything great?" I asked.

Ben read over the options. I felt lucky that I could be picky and only take jobs that spoke to me in some way, and of course stayed in line with Mom's "nothing too dangerous" rule. Big horse race in Maryland? Not so interested. Sixteen-year-old matador facing six bulls in one day? Very interested, but the magazine wanted a *pro*-bullfighting angle, and I couldn't be part of that. Success of a once homeless woman who turned her life around by using microloans to start her own business? Loved it; big, resounding yes.

"That's about it." Ben shrugged, then looked down again at his list as if he'd just noticed something. "Oh, wait—there's one more thing . . . any desire to go to Carnival in Rio?"

He tried to keep a straight face, but he couldn't pull it off.

My jaw dropped. "Are you kidding me? YES!!!"

There were about a million reasons I wanted to go to Carnival. Not only was it a massive four-day celebration unlike anything else in the world, but it was also a photojournalist's dream: ornate costumes, wild revelry, and throngs of people from every walk of life, surging into the streets to rejoice together.

Of course, I also had a personal reason to go to Brazil. For a year now, I'd wanted to visit the place where my father had disappeared. I wanted to talk to the people who'd been with him in his last days. Mom thought the idea was pointless and morbid. She had already been in touch with everyone at the GloboReach camp outside of Rio, where Dad had last been seen. She spoke to them on the phone the day he was declared missing and went there in person almost immediately thereafter. Everyone told her the same story: that Dad's time at the camp was just like all his other visits. He saw patients, he counseled other doctors, he surveyed the operations to see how the outpost could work even better. Had there been drama or violence? Sure, that was a way of life in the *favelas,* the poorest parts of Rio; but the drama and violence had been nothing out of the ordinary, and nothing that had to do with Dad himself.

Dad *had* gone off alone on a few occasions, and he hadn't let anyone know where he was going. But this wasn't unusual. He always became personally invested in his patients' lives, and it was common for him to visit former patients whenever he returned to a GloboReach camp. He'd also get so engrossed in individuals' stories that he'd embark on one-man missions, striving to accomplish that little bit more to help a certain family or village. Given all that, no one thought twice about Dad being away and out of touch until several days had gone by. At that point the trail had already run cold, and no amount of Weston family money or powerful government emissaries could change that.

Four months went by between Dad's disappearance and the official declaration of his death. In that time my mom's mind-set decayed from fierce certitude that her money and connections would find my father, to a determined hope that they could at least bring her answers, to abject despair about everything in the universe. She survived only by closing the door on the whole thing. She was afraid that if I opened it back up, I'd be leaping back into the same world of pain.

Mom didn't realize I'd never *left* that world. The only thing I thought might help me escape was to get some answers of my own, even if those answers were the same things I'd already heard through Mom, and even if they killed the last tiny fire of hope I held that my dad could maybe, possibly, somehow still be alive.

"Think she'll sign the paper?" Ben asked as I pulled out my cell phone and dialed. Since my eighteenth birthday was still a couple of months away, I needed a notarized permission letter from my mother each time I traveled outside the country.

Not every airport asked for it, but many did, and it was technically a requirement. If they asked when I got to customs in Brazil and I didn't have it, they wouldn't let me out of the airport. I'd have to take the next flight home.

Mom wasn't answering. I left her a message with all the pertinent information, and asked her to call me.

"You know she won't want you to go," Ben said.

"I know. But it's for work. I think she'll give in." I nodded toward the playing cards. "You want to deal, or would you rather postpone your agony?"

"Big talk from somebody about to be double-skunked."

"Ooooh. Cocky much?"

Ben just grinned and dealt. We left Dalt's several hours later, with our cribbage game tally dead even.

My phone rang on the drive back home.

"Shalom," I chirped to my mom. "Isn't it the middle of the night in Israel?"

"I don't think it's a good idea, Clea."

I could hear the roar of laughter and loud conversation behind her and knew she'd stepped away from a dinner party; the kind that seemed casual and friendly, but at which many of her greatest political accomplishments were hatched. She wanted to cut to the chase; she wouldn't be able to stay on the phone very long.

"It's a legitimate assignment," I said.

"The one you were hired for, or the one you'll actually do?"

"I will absolutely do the job I was hired to do."

An explosion of laughter erupted from the crowd. Mom joined in.

"We'll talk later," she said. "Love you."

She clicked off, and I smiled. She hadn't said no. I turned up my radio and continued home, stopping by Rayna's house to munch popcorn and catch up on the TiVo'd shows we'd missed. It was late by the time I hung the cribbage board back on my wall and climbed into bed, and I imagined for once I'd easily fall asleep.

I was right. I did fall asleep. But then the dreams came.

The room was in shades of red, which matched the robe I wore. I sat in front of a mirror, slathering cold cream onto my face to loosen the thick stage makeup.

There was a knock at the door. Three raps fast, then two slow. Our signal. I eagerly rose to unlock the door, taking care not to make a sound. I didn't want him to enter before I was ready. I sat back down and quickly blotted the extra cream off my face. I turned down the wick on my table lamp, then called, "Come in."

I didn't turn to look at him, but our eyes met through the mirror. We'd been together for a year now, but seeing him still made me nervous. He was the most beautiful man I had ever seen. Not that he looked perfect. His nose bulged slightly near the top, like it had been broken ages ago and hadn't quite healed properly. And though he was young, ever-so-thin lines snaked out from the corners of his eyes. They gave him character; he looked like a man who'd wrestled with life and won.

"What took you so long?" he asked as he removed his top hat and ducked his muscular frame through the door. "I was worried."

I wheeled in my seat, primed to snap, but he was smiling. I relaxed and laughed. He was teasing me. I always said he worried about me far too much and it would be the death of me, so now he was playing it up on purpose. "You are so bad," I said.

"And you," he said, holding out a huge bouquet of red irises, "were so, so good."

"Did you really like it?"

"Hamlet has never had a better Ophelia."

"In over two hundred years?" I asked. "I'm not sure you're qualified to make that statement."

His mouth curled in a wry half smile. "Oh, I'm pretty sure I am."

I rolled my eyes and gave him the closed-lip smile I almost always used when I wasn't onstage.

He didn't let me get away with it. "You know I think your smile is beautiful, Anneline."

I blushed. He knew I hated the little gap between my front teeth. I could forget about it when I was in character, but in real life it felt like a sinkhole in the middle of my face.

"You're so convinced you'll disappoint people if you show them that you're not perfect," he said gently.

I blinked back the tears that suddenly welled behind my eyes. He always knew the deeper truth behind what I did, even when it was something so scary and personal that I'd never say it out loud to anyone, even myself.

"You don't realize you *are* perfect," he went on. "Your imperfections are what make you perfect. They make you *you*. That's what people love. It's what I love too."

I had to blink harder now to stop the tears, but

they were tears of gratitude. It had been that way from the day we met—like he could see every place my heart was cracked and would pull open the wounds, inspect them, dig out every bit of infection, then fill them with his love until they healed.

It felt so good I almost couldn't take it. I smiled—a real smile—and quickly changed the subject. I nodded to the bouquet of irises in his hand, then to the vase of long-stemmed roses on my dressing room table, "Roses *and* irises? You're feeling extravagant today."

He shook his head. "I didn't send you those."

"No? The note says 'From Your Biggest Fan.' They were delivered before the show started. They aren't from you?"

"I know you prefer irises." He held up the bouquet. "May I?"

"Of course."

He pulled the roses from the vase so he could replace them with his own bouquet, but he winced and immediately dropped all the flowers.

"Are you okay?" I asked.

"Thorns," he said, grimacing. Several blooms of blood pearled on his hand, quickly growing in size. He clenched his fist against the sting.

"I'll get you a cloth."

"Don't. I'm fine."

"Martyr." I pulled a cloth from a drawer, then took his clenched hand in mine. "Open up."

"Anneline, I'm fine."

"Open."

He did . . . and his hand was unscathed.

"How . . . what happened?" I asked.

"The bleeding stopped."

"No," I said, running my thumb over his open palm and fingers. "There's nothing here. Not even a scratch."

"I was barely even cut."

"You were bleeding all over your hand," I insisted. I pushed down on his palm. No red blossoms pooled into view. Nothing.

"Ow!" He laughed. "Are you *trying* to make me bleed?" He closed his hand over mine, and with his other hand tipped my face up until my eyes met his. "I'm fine," he assured me. "I'm better than fine. At least, I could be . . ."

Still holding my hand, he sank to one knee and pulled a small box from his pocket.

No. It couldn't be.

He opened the box to reveal a single perfect diamond on a delicate ring. He looked up at me, and I saw an eternity of love in his eyes. "Will you marry me, Anneline?"

I saw it all in that second; our entire lives sprawling out ahead of us, a whirlwind of images whizzing so fast I couldn't grab a single one, but the feeling of them broke over me in a wave of happiness so pure it made me cry.

"Anneline?" His eyes widened in concern.

"Yes! Yes, I'll marry you!"

He didn't say anything, but his smile glowed as he got to his feet and scooped me into his arms. I screamed and laughed and cried, and my whole world became an ecstatic blur. . . .

I sat up in bed, breathless and dizzy. I spun my head toward my computer, irrationally positive the man would be there, stepping out of the darkened screen.

He wasn't, of course, but I had to see him. I rolled out of bed, but I was still too hazy from the dream to get my footing, and thumped onto the floor. Instantly there was a bang on my door.

"What happened in there?" Piri asked.

"I'm fine!" I called. "Just a bad dream."

The door flung open.

"A bad dream?" Piri tsked with alarm. "Someone

walking over your grave. Wear your clothes inside out today; turn your luck around."

She stared at me, waiting for me to give the absurd superstition its due respect.

"Sure, I'll do that, Piri. Thanks."

Piri nodded, then shut the door. Before it closed all the way, I saw her gaze at Dad's office door and cross herself. I rolled my eyes.

I got up and contemplated my computer. Only a moment ago I'd been desperate to turn it on and see the man from my dreams, but suddenly I wasn't sure. I tried to tell myself the same thing I had the night before, that vivid fantasies about the man were my brain's way of making him less scary and easier to deal with. I even thought about what Rayna would say: The man was mysterious and beautiful—it would be stranger if I *didn't* fantasize about him. She'd tell me it was harmless, and I should just thank my imagination for a good night's fun.

The problem was that these dreams didn't feel fun. They felt thick and real, and they clung to me like moss, leaving me disoriented and weirdly out of control. I didn't like it, and I had a feeling that the more time I spent looking at the pictures, the more vivid the dreams would become. I'd be better off avoiding them, maybe until after Rio. By then I imagined enough time would have passed that they might not have such a grip on me.

It seemed like a good plan . . . but the dreams kept coming. Every time I closed my eyes, I dove into another chapter of the love story between myself and this man. Only I was never really *me*. I was Delia, or Anneline, or Catherine, or Olivia—always one of those four women, each of whom lived in a different era. And the visions felt less like dreams and more like being flung backward through time.

At first I hated it. No matter how happy I was within the dreams themselves, I woke up feeling like my brain had been hijacked by the guy in the pictures. I tried to fight against the dreams. I'd purposely fall asleep in front of the scariest or most dramatic movies, hoping they'd suck me into their stories while I slept. I'd download visualization exercises specifically made to help you shape your own dreams. I'd run on the treadmill for miles at night until I was sure I'd hit the pillow too exhausted to dream at all.

Nothing worked. Every night I was back in time again. I was Olivia in Renaissance Italy, trying to perfect my watercolor technique by painting the man I loved and his best friend Giovanni. They were terrible models; they couldn't stay still for more than two minutes without cracking each other up. Other nights I lived a hundred years later, as Catherine in rural England, racing bareback through the countryside, the man from the pictures pushing his horse to keep up with me. Other nights Anneline swept me onto France's finest nineteenth-century stages, or Delia whisked me to Prohibition-era Chicago.

I got so frustrated, I almost called my therapist to tell her about it, but something wouldn't let me do it. I hated how helpless I was to fight the dreams, but I also felt weirdly protective of them. They were mine. The man was mine. I didn't want to share them with anyone. I couldn't explain why I felt that way, but I did.

After a full week, something even stranger happened: I stopped feeling irritated that I couldn't control the dreams, and started looking forward to them. It didn't happen all at once, but the more time I spent with the man, the more I started falling for him, and the less it mattered that I wasn't in control.

He had a way about him. No matter how much I tried to protect myself and hide, he always saw through to the core of what I was truly feeling. And while he was technically performing this magic with four other women, as long as I was asleep those women were *me*. They looked like me (with the exception of the small gap between my teeth when I was Anneline), they sounded like me, and they had the same deep-seated, unspoken fears that we were all desperately afraid to show.

Those fears didn't faze the man at all. In fact, he loved me for them, and for the quirks I developed to try and cover them up. It was like he was made for me. He made me feel safe and loved in a way no man ever had in real life. He was even marked as mine. At least, I liked to think of it that way. His chest was stamped with a small tattoo . . . a tattoo in the shape of an iris.

In the end, I didn't care if the dreams were fantasies; they were impossible to resist. I started making excuses to go to bed earlier and earlier, and even took midday naps to satisfy the part of me that couldn't wait to be with him. Waking up was heartbreaking. Each time I sat up in bed and realized I was alone, I felt as if part of me had been ripped away. I clung to the wisps of the dreams as long as I could, but they always faded too soon, leaving me sad and empty and wanting more. Daydreams about him didn't have the same tactile feel of reality, but since they were all I had to try to fill the void between sleeps, they had to be enough.

"That's it," Rayna said, pushing my laptop closed. It was about a week before the Rio trip, and she and I were at the kitchen island working on term papers.

"Rayna!" I complained. "I could've lost my work!"

"Please. You hadn't typed anything in the last hour. Consider this a one-person intervention: Who is he and why haven't you told me about him?"

I felt the blush rise into my face. "Who is who?"

"Seriously? You're going to play that with me? Clea, it's obvious. You're practically delirious; you've been a million miles away since we got back from—" She gasped and smacked my arm. "Oh! My! *God!* It's Ben, isn't it? I *did* interrupt something the night we got back from Paris. It's Ben, and you haven't told me because you didn't want me to say I told you so, when I *so* told you so! You *loser*!" She hurled the epithet with a grin of such complete delight that I almost hated to tell her the truth.

"No! Rayna, it's not Ben. It's not anyone."

"Liar."

"Okay, it's not anyone *real,*" I said, grimacing.

She was still glaring at me skeptically. There was no way I'd get out of the conversation without telling her something. And the truth was that as much as I wanted to keep the man to myself, I was also bubbling over about him inside, and part of me was dying to dish about him with my best girlfriend. Still, I wasn't exactly sure about the best way to start dishing about someone who existed only in my dreams.

I took a deep breath and just dove in. I told her all about the dreams, but I didn't mention how I first saw him. I just said he was some guy I'd seen in a picture somewhere.

It actually felt great to talk about him. I felt like I gushed for ages. When I was done, Rayna just stared at me.

"You know what I'm going to say, don't you?" she asked.

"I need a boyfriend."

"You do need a boyfriend."

"I don't need a boyfriend."

Rayna raised an eyebrow.

"I don't *need* a boyfriend," I clarified. "I'm not

saying I'm against the idea, but I don't want someone just to have someone. It has to be the right person."

"And Make-Believe-Fantasy-Guy is the right person?"

Yes! He is! I wanted to shout . . . but that would have sounded crazy. Still, it felt completely, 100 percent true. The man in my dreams *was* the right person. He proved it to me every night.

Of course he did. No matter how real the dreams felt, they were *dreams*, which meant the man's personality was a figment of my imagination. Of course he knew me better than anyone else! Why wouldn't I make him perfect for me? The iris tattoo was an especially nice touch, tying him in with my father and how horribly I missed him. Freud would have had a field day with it.

Yet no matter how obvious all that was, it didn't change my feelings. I shut my mouth and let Rayna think she had won the argument. I even told her she could fix me up with someone after I got back from Rio, though I knew no one would match up to the man I'd created in my mind.

Three days later it was Ben who cornered me. We were at Dalt's, and I was finishing off a blueberry muffin—grilled, of course—while we played cribbage and I daydreamed.

"So when the pod people come and steal your body, does it hurt, or are you pretty much unconscious for the whole thing?"

"Huh?" I asked.

"I just double-skunked you three times in a row. What's going on with you?"

He lifted an eyebrow. He was in detective mode now, and there was no escaping it. I imagined spilling to him the way I had to Rayna, and almost choked. I'd rather die than describe my fantasies to Ben. I'd never hear the end of it.

Still, I needed to tell him something, and he knew me too well to buy a complete lie.

I thought about the pictures. I could tell him about the pictures without telling him about the dreams. Ben was like Dad—he ate up anything that smacked of the inexplicable. He'd probably love the picture of the man at St. Vitus's Cathedral, standing in midair on nothing.

"You might think I'm crazy . . . ," I started.

"I already think that, so . . ."

I took a deep breath, then started to explain. I told him about every picture, including the ones that were completely impossible and seemed to prove the man wasn't actually in the shots when I snapped them. By the time I finished, Ben's brow was furrowed, and the concern in his eyes had deepened into alarm.

He really did think I was crazy. I shouldn't have told him.

"Can you stop looking at me like that? I know there's a logical explanation," I assured him. "I just don't know what it is yet, but—"

"You need to show me those pictures," Ben said gravely.

"Um . . . okay," I said, though I suddenly wasn't positive I wanted to share them. "After Rio I figured I'd open them up again and try to—"

"Now, Clea," he said. "I really need to see them now."

four

TWENTY MINUTES LATER Ben was in my room, leaning heavily on my desk, one hand twined in his front tuft of hair as he stared at my computer screen. I clicked through each picture, first as I had originally composed it, then with the enlarged view showcasing my fantasy man. Seeing him on the screen was more intense than I'd thought it would be—my heart started pounding so hard I could feel it in my head, and I worried Ben could hear it.

I glanced toward him to check, but he wasn't looking at me. His eyes were locked on the screen.

"Mind if I steer?" he asked tightly, his hand poised over the mouse. I never let anyone else drive my computer and Ben knew it, but at the moment it took all my energy to keep myself together. I nodded, and he took the mouse, clicking through the photos and zooming even closer on the man's profile, his eyes, his lips. . . .

I shuddered. This had to stop. I wasn't acting like myself at all, and I had no good explanation to give Ben if he asked me why.

"Clea," he said.

I winced, preparing for the most embarrassing conversation of my life, but Ben looked exhausted, like the last ten minutes had utterly drained him. He drew his hand out of his hair, then looked at me apologetically. "I need to show you something downstairs."

"You do?" I couldn't imagine what he would need to show me in my own house, but I followed him down two flights of stairs. Then he turned toward my dad's studio.

"Ben . . . ," I warned.

"I know. But we have to go in."

I strained against the urge to howl and pull him away as he opened the door. The studio had been my dad's inner sanctum. For as long as I could remember, the rule was that you either went in with Dad, or you knocked and waited for permission. Time in the studio was a by-invitation-only honor to be shared with Dad, which meant the door had stayed closed for the last year. Entering without him now felt like a desecration.

"He'd want you to, Clea," Ben said. "Believe me."

For the first time, I felt a little flare of anger toward Ben. Grant Raymond was *my* dad. Why would Ben know what he'd want better than me? I was about to work up a suitably snarky reply, but Ben's ghost white face stopped me. Something was very wrong, and for some reason he needed to tell me in the studio. I went in.

Like Dad's office, his studio was a maelstrom of loose papers, books, and a spectrum of supplies. Yet while the office drowned in work chaos, the studio exulted in the wilder bedlam of his amusements. Digital photography was king among these, and no less than three large computer monitors rose like islands among the reams of photo paper, extra ink cartridges, and tangles of USB cords. Everywhere sat much-loved and dog-eared tomes of mythology and history from all over the world.

In the middle of one stack of books I noticed

a biography of William Shakespeare, and I felt a pang of heartbreak. I missed my dad so much. I hated to think that even my smallest memories of him were fading, and yet I had almost completely forgotten how passionate he'd become about Shakespeare about six months before he disappeared. Mom had been stunned by it. She had spent years begging Dad to accompany her to the theater. Then all of a sudden he was ravenously devouring everything even remotely Bard-related: plays, sonnets, and volumes of commentary on his works. That was Dad's way. When he seized on a new topic, he studied it exhaustively.

Ben opened the closet where Dad kept all his cameras, from his newest digitals to collectors-item Brownies he'd bought on eBay, to long-defunct Polaroid OneSteps he couldn't bear to throw away. I winced as Ben shifted them around and they clanked together.

"Be careful," I said.

"Sorry. Almost got it."

He pushed aside a couple more cameras, then stood on tiptoe and leaned forward to press a spot against the back wall. What was he doing?

"There," he said.

"Where? What are you talking about?"

He didn't answer, just grabbed a step stool and carried it to the far wall of the room, which was covered in framed photographs. Many were shots Dad had taken himself, like the eight-by-ten of my big, round, three-month-old smiling face. Others were my handiwork, like the girl with the prosthetic leg breaking the tape on her first cross-country race.

But as Ben climbed the step stool, I noticed that one of those framed photos had hinged open, popping out slightly from its place on the wall. It was a picture of two decrepit and crumbling vials, half-buried in dirt—the items that had made Dad a rock star with all the New Agers. Entire websites and fan forums were dedicated to these vials: "The Ancient Vials of the Elixir of Life."

My father had set up and funded the dig to find the vials, and had gone to Italy to personally supervise the work. When they were actually unearthed, even the mainstream media carried the news. They were, however, quick to add that while the containers were indeed very old, very like their reputed description, and very archaeologically significant, they were also very empty. No Elixir of Life. Dad wasn't concerned. He was thrilled with the discovery and must have taken hundreds of pictures of them before turning them over to the Museo Nazionale Romano.

Now one of those pictures was a gateway to a secret compartment Ben knew all about . . . but I had no idea even existed. Ben pulled the door open the rest of the way and tugged out a wildly overstuffed folder. He joined me at the long table Dad had used as his work space, pushed clear an area, and thumped the folder down.

Pictures. The engorged folder held a massive stack of pictures.

"Why did your dad tell you he hired me?" Ben asked.

"For your knowledge," I replied.

"My knowledge," he mused. "That's why your mom hired me. Your dad wasn't as interested in what I knew. He hired me for what I *didn't* know . . . but still believed."

"I have absolutely no idea what that means. What does that mean?"

Ben took a deep breath and ran his hands through his hair again, grabbing it as if he could pull the right words out of his head. "There are things beyond human understanding," he said, and I didn't know if he was trying to quote my father or doing it inadvertently. "Things we have to accept, because we can never explain them. Your dad believed that, and it was important to him that I do too."

I knew Dad and Ben both loved all things otherworldly. That was no surprise—I'd rolled my eyes through tons of their late-night conversations. But Ben was saying that Dad *required* Ben to believe in those things as part of his job, which was weird. "Why?" I asked.

"So I could protect you," he said. He opened the folder. "Recognize this?" he asked, nodding to the photo on the top.

"Of course," I said. It was the day Mom, Wanda, Rayna, and I had left the hospital almost eighteen years ago. We were in the reception area on the way out: Mom and Wanda in their wheelchairs, newborns Rayna and I in our mothers' laps.

"See all the people in the background?" Ben asked.

I nodded. Dad himself had admitted he'd been too excited to frame the shot properly. The four of us were low in the foreground, with the rest of the picture full of random people.

"Your dad enlarged the picture to check them out. He said he didn't know why, he just felt like he needed to do it."

Ben flipped to the next picture. It was the same shot, but the strangers in the reception area were larger now, more in focus. I could even see the hallway beyond reception: vague shapes of nurses pushing a stretcher and other figures.

"See anything familiar?" Ben asked.

I shook my head. I didn't, but I could imagine where this was going, and my stomach had balled into a knot of anticipation.

Ben pursed his lips grimly and flipped to the next image. "How about now?" he asked.

A wave of dizziness washed over me, and I clutched the counter to steady myself.

He was there.

The man from my dreams.

He was in that back hall, standing by the elevators. The image was grainy, but it was unmistakably him. And though it was almost eighteen years ago, he looked exactly the same as he did in my pictures. Not a day's difference. He even wore the same thing: a black leather jacket over jeans and a gray T-shirt.

"Your dad said he couldn't explain it—there was just something about the guy . . . something that wasn't right."

I studied the picture. The man was far from my

mother and me, but he was looking in our direction, and he didn't look happy. His back was a little hunched, his hands were sunk deep into his pockets, and his eyes looked like he might have been crying.

Ben looked at me as if waiting for a response, but I didn't know what to say.

"He looks sad," I finally forced out.

Ben nodded. "Not the strangest thing for someone at a hospital, but your dad couldn't shake the idea that the guy wasn't sad about anyone else, but about *you*. It was just a feeling, but he believed it, and he told me that for a while, he enlarged and investigated every single picture he took. He figured if his feeling was right, the guy would show up again. It didn't happen, and your dad said he realized he was being crazy. He had to work, he wanted time with you and your mom . . . he couldn't spend every spare hour down here chasing phantoms."

Ben glanced at me, knowing I'd normally chide him for the word. This time I didn't.

"Grant told me that when you were about four months old, he was working with some JPEGs when he had that feeling again, and . . ."

Instead of explaining, Ben simply flipped to the

next picture. It was some kind of formal event. Circular tables were laid out in fine linens and china, and Mom wore a black cocktail dress, high heels . . . and me, strapped to her chest in a Baby Bjorn. I remembered this picture too. Mom loved to tell me how she took me everywhere when I was an infant. She said voters went crazy for the way she proved she could be completely devoted to both her newborn and her career. Sure enough, she was working it in the picture, shaking hands with the vice president of the United States as his wife and I gave each other big, goofy grins.

Now well aware of what I was really looking for, I gave Mom and myself only a cursory glance before surveying the background. It didn't take long.

"There," I whispered, pointing to a seat several tables away from my mom's. The image was small, but . . .

"Exactly," Ben said, moving to the next shot, which was of course an enlargement of the very spot I had just identified. The man faced mostly away from the camera. His elbows rested on the table, his right fist balled against his temple. He looked wildly out of place, his leather jacket and jeans standing in stark relief against the gowns and tuxedos of everyone else.

"Tough to miss in that crowd," Ben said, echoing what I'd been thinking, "but your dad said he never saw him there. No one did; your dad asked around. Eventually he came to the same conclusion you did, when you took the pictures of your room: The guy was never actually there."

"Didn't *seem* to be there," I clarified, "but there has to be some kind of logical explanation. Quantum physics, even—something we don't really understand. . . ."

Ben just shrugged, and flipped through more pictures: pictures of me as a toddler, a child, a tween . . . always a regular photo followed by an enlargement that featured the same ageless man. "Your dad said he was really worried at first," Ben continued as he turned over picture after picture, "especially since he had to keep it to himself. He knew your mom would think he was crazy. By the time you were a little kid and nothing horrible had happened, though, he was still pretty confused, but he wasn't as anxious about it."

"Wait," I said, putting my hand on the pile of pictures. "This one's mine."

It had been my first truly successful print, and I took it on my eighth birthday. We were on Kauai, and all I'd wanted was a horseback ride along the beach at dusk. Mom was thrilled, and as we all rode I'd snapped a perfect shot of Mom, Dad, and Rayna on horseback, silhouetted by the hot pink setting sun.

"I know," Ben said. "Your dad told me he wondered if this guy would show up in pictures *you* took, so every now and then he'd search through your shots. Sure enough . . ."

Ben turned to the next picture: an enlargement of the one I knew so well, but centered on the ocean far beyond my mom, Dad, and Rayna. There was an outcropping of rocks in the water. Sitting among their crags and ridges was the man.

It took an eternity to find my voice. "So this guy, this . . ." I almost repeated Ben's "phantom," but the word stuck in my throat. "He's been in my pictures forever?"

Ben nodded. "Pictures of you and pictures you took. Not all of them, but probably a lot more than these. Your dad just found the ones that grabbed him somehow, like the ones from your trip grabbed you."

"But all this time . . . how did I not notice?"

"Don't know. Maybe it wasn't ready for you to notice it."

"It?"

Ben rummaged through the volumes in Dad's jam-packed bookcase, then pulled out a massive tome with a cracked red leather cover and pages soft with wear.

"What is this?" I asked as it thumped onto the table. The cover had no title, only a large embossed circle.

"You won't like it," Ben warned. "The circle is an ancient symbol of never-ending life. The book is a guide to the spirit world. Your dad thought it might have some answers."

I looked at Ben askance, but he just nodded toward the book. I opened it gently. The pages had been hand-bound—they were all slightly different sizes, and the type wasn't completely straight on the page. The old-style calligraphy was thick and difficult to read, and almost completely overshadowed by the hand-drawn borders and illustrations. I flipped to a bookmarked page, most of which glowed with the image of a rapturously beautiful winged man. His wings were spread wide, and he smiled down protectively at an infant in a basket. There was a small Post-it next to the infant, and Dad had scrawled on it: "Clea???"

I looked at Ben.

"Can you make out the heading?" he asked.

I studied the ornate script.

"Guardian Angel?" I asked.

Ben nodded. "That was Grant's hope, that the man was your guardian angel, protecting you from harm."

I smiled, thinking of how protective he had always been in my dreams. "That makes sense," I mused, then quickly added, "In a this-is-all-insane-and-impossible kind of way."

Ben tilted his head noncommittally. "Your dad wasn't convinced."

He nodded back toward the book, and I noticed another bookmark. I flipped to the page and gasped. This one too was filled mainly with an illustration of a winged man, but this man was rendered in shades of red. He had the body of a god, but his face was monstrous, and he leered down at an innocent-looking sleeping woman, his arms spread wide and every muscle taut with coiled rage as he prepared to spring.

Again Dad had affixed a Post-it to the page, this one near the sleeping woman, but his scrawl was smaller and cowed. "Clea . . . ?" it wondered.

I gazed at the heading. I'd heard the word, but I had a strong feeling that in this context it had nothing to do with music. "Incubus?" I asked Ben.

He nodded grimly. "A lost soul—usually male—turned evil spirit that attaches itself to someone in order to lead her astray. The spirit is kind of . . . sexual in nature." He reddened and gestured to the picture. "Like it shows there. The incubus comes to a woman and has . . . you know . . . relations with her in her sleep."

My jaw dropped, and I was glad Ben's eyes were averted as an exhilarating stream of images from my dreams flashed at super-speed through my head. I didn't realize I'd been holding my breath until it came out in a whoosh that I tried to pass off as a laugh.

"It's not funny, Clea."

"It's *insane*. Even if there were such a thing as an evil spirit, wouldn't it be obvious if I'd spent my whole life stalked by one? Wouldn't terrible things have happened to me?"

"Maybe they will. Maybe he's just been waiting for the right time. Maybe that time is now, and that's why all of a sudden you see him everywhere."

"So he's a *patient* evil spirit," I said sarcastically.

"Know what else comes from the same Latin root as 'incubus'?" Ben retorted. "*Incubate*. I don't think it's coincidence. I think this . . . thing has been incubating, and now it's ready to come out and do whatever it's going to do. And I think your dad would agree with me."

"You have no idea what my dad would think," I shot back jealously . . . but I knew that wasn't true. In the last half hour Ben had proven he knew my dad far better than I had ever realized . . . maybe far better than I'd known him myself.

Ben reached up to twine his fingers in his hair, then drew them out. "I'm sorry. I know this is a lot. It's just . . . this is the real reason your dad hired me. Once you started traveling, he knew you'd be away a lot, and he wanted someone around who knew all this and could keep an eye out for anything strange. He worried about you. I worry about you too."

He *was* worried; I could see it in his eyes. Whether or not I could buy into his and Dad's theories about the man in the pictures, I knew for sure they both only wanted to protect me, and that was something I had to respect.

"Okay," I said. "So what do you think we should do?"

"I think we should skip the trip to Rio."

"Are you crazy? Why? What does one thing have to do with the other?"

"Maybe nothing," Ben admitted, "but Rio wasn't exactly the safest place in the world for your dad. If this thing is getting ready to make some kind of move, I don't think we should make it easier by going someplace dangerous."

"If you really believe the 'thing' isn't human, it shouldn't matter where I am, right? He can make a move in my own bedroom."

Bad choice of words. I felt myself redden, and quickly moved on.

"Besides, Dad *also* thought the guy could be my guardian angel. Are you forgetting that?"

"Does he look like a guardian angel?"

He did *not* look like a guardian angel, but everything I knew about him made me believe he couldn't possibly be evil.

Of course, everything I knew about him—no matter how real it felt—was just a figment of my imagination . . . wasn't it?

Just like guardian angels and incubi were figments of the imagination.

I had to get back to dealing with facts. One fact was that something bizarre was going on, but I'd be far more likely to find an explanation in a modern book on string theory than in an ancient tome on the spirit world. The other fact was that my whole life, Dad had apparently known this bizarre thing was going on, and had neglected to tell the one person most obviously impacted by it.

"Why did my dad tell *you* about these pictures and not me?" I asked.

"We talked about that. He told me that when you were little he didn't want to scare you. And when you were older, you were too much like your mom and would never believe him."

I smiled. Dad was right, and in that moment I felt like he was with us in the room. I also realized something—I *did* know him better than Ben did. I knew what he would think.

"Dad knew about this thing my whole life," I said, "but he never let it get in the way of what I wanted to do. I can't either. We're going to Rio."

Ben opened his mouth to object, but he knew better. He just sighed.

"Okay . . . we're going to Rio."

That evening a FedEx envelope arrived from my mom, containing the notarized permission I needed for the flight to Brazil. She included a note with it: *I still don't like it, but I trust you'll make the choice that's right for you. Love, Mom.*

The trip was on.

As I went to bed that night, I couldn't help but

wonder if what I'd learned would change what happened in my dreams. Would the man still be there? Would he act the same? I was dying to know, but unfortunately it turns out it's almost impossible to fall asleep when you're actively chasing a specific dream. By two in the morning I'd given up and was playing solitaire in bed while watching an old sitcom on TV. I'd planned to pad downstairs the minute the show ended and make a pot of tea, but it never happened.

Instead I found myself sitting at Dalt's.

I was at the counter, watching the cook flip several burgers and a large apple pie on the grill. The door squeaked open, and though I didn't even raise my eyes, I knew it was him. I felt the air change when he entered, the force of him as he strode across the diner, and the heat of his body mere inches from mine as he sat.

Electricity leaped between us, and his eyes burned into me, but I still wouldn't turn to face him.

"Who are you?" I asked.

"You know who I am," he replied. "I'm yours."

The cook expertly flipped a burger and pressed it down with his spatula. The meat sizzled and spluttered in the grease.

"Should I be frightened?" I asked.

"Why bother?" he replied. "It'll all end the same."

The cook slid a plate in front of me: a hot, juicy burger, shining greasily on an open-faced bun.

Only it wasn't a burger at all. It was a grilled tarantula.

I gasped and looked up at the cook. It was Ben, beads of sweat dripping from his forehead. He winked and pointed his spatula to the grill, where six more huge spiders spluttered and sizzled away.

Horrified, I turned away . . . and came face-to-face with the man, his eyes as deep and intoxicating as ever . . . only now they stared out at me from a rotting skull.

"Kiss me," he hissed. I wanted to run, but I couldn't move, and as the creature leaned toward me and unhinged its horrible mouth, I saw inside an endless swirling mass of inky black nothingness I knew would pull me closer and closer until I drowned inside. . . .

I bolted upright in bed and realized with horror that there was something clinging to my face. I clawed wildly at it and scratched away . . .

. . . a playing card.

"Ugh!" I groaned, tossing it aside.

So my dreamtime love was now the stuff of nightmares. Good. Better, really. I'd have more perspective that way.

But the nightmares didn't last. Nor did my regular romantic fantasies come back. The two somehow morphed together. For the next two nights I was plagued by far more terrible dreams, dreams that were sticky with reality, but a terrible, disjointed reality, where nothing made sense, but it was all incredibly vivid.

I was Olivia. I was in a beautiful room that glowed like the sun. A circle of others were with me, all of them draped in clothing so bright that it hurt my eyes.

He was with me, holding my hand. He smiled . . . then blood started pouring out of his chest, his arms, his legs . . . gushing and running down his body, but he seemed to have no idea. He kept smiling, and he gave my hand a comforting squeeze. I screamed, but he didn't seem to notice.

I looked around for help, but all I saw were the two decrepit, half-buried vials from my dad's archaeological dig. A raven-haired woman with dancing black eyes picked up the vials and held them out to me, laughing wildly as a long cut opened up in her throat and blood began to flow. I turned away from the sight and came face-to-face with Giovanni, my love's best friend.

"Giovanni!" I cried. "Help me! Help us!"

"Shh," he said, a finger to his lips. "It's better this way . . . it's all for the best."

I didn't understand—what was for the best? I was desperate for answers, but he didn't say a word. I didn't even see the heavy object he picked up until it came barreling toward my head.

The next night was stranger and even more surreal. I was Anneline. It was my wedding day, and I walked down the aisle toward the man, grinning for all I was worth. I was almost at his side when I realized the man walking me down the aisle wasn't my father, but Ben.

Actually, not Ben. He seemed like Ben, but he looked different. Broader. Taller? Julien. His name was Julien. He stopped me just before I reached my fiancé. Smiling down at me, he pulled out a long-stemmed rose . . . and pushed it gently through my dress, adding the littlest bit of pressure to pierce it into my heart.

I gasped as I felt the thorns slice my flesh and slide through my body.

"Julien . . . !"

He kept smiling, and steered me to the altar. No one seemed to notice the rose impaling me. The guests, the priests, my groom—everyone smiled peacefully as the ceremony continued and I struggled to breathe, blood now spreading across my white dress. As the priest spoke, Julien pulled out another rose.

"No," I begged, but he didn't listen. He studied me closely, then threaded this flower through my body, arranging it perfectly next to the other.

I stood there at the altar, gripping my bloodstained bouquet of white irises, looking desperately for help to everyone around me, but no one paid attention, not even when I hit the floor and faded into nothingness. . . .

It was terrible. In just a few nights I had gone from craving my dreams to dreading them. Even when I woke up, I couldn't shake the gummy horror of the visions, and I started feeling like my regular life was the fantasy, and the gut-wrenching dreams were real life.

What was happening to me?

five

WHATEVER WAS HAPPENING, there was absolutely no way I could let myself fall asleep during the twelve-hour trip to Rio with Ben. He was already freaked out about the pictures—if he saw me flailing and crying in my sleep, he'd lose it. Or worse, the other dreams could come back—the ones so good I could feel every touch. I could only imagine what I looked like when I dreamed those. No way could I let Ben see that. I'd die.

I didn't close my eyes during the trip, and I was exhausted by the time we landed. I followed Ben in a zombielike daze as we got our luggage, rented a Jeep, drove to the hotel, checked in, and split off to our separate rooms. The bed looked so good, but the people at GloboReach were expecting us, so I reluctantly changed and got ready to go.

Outside the hotel, I breathed in the salty air and let Rio bring me back to life. Its energy was palpable: The beach teemed with wealthy tourists in designer bikinis and sunglasses, and the wide streets swarmed with local musicians and people waiting eagerly for that night's Samba Parade—the highlight of Carnival.

Ben drove the Jeep. I kicked back my seat, slipped off my shoes, and rested my feet on the dash, letting my limbs bask in the baking sun as we drove to the outpost. There had been snow on the ground when we left Connecticut; here it was ninety degrees. Despite everything, I felt light and free in my cutoff shorts, white tank top, and sunglasses, liberated from the ten pounds of coats and sweaters I'd been wearing at home.

The GloboReach camp where my dad had last been seen was just outside one of the more notorious *favelas*, the slums outside the city. It wasn't far from our hotel, but it was a world away. As we got closer, the streets grew narrow and unpaved, and I could almost feel the looming sense of violence my dad had told me was so rampant here. He'd said it was bizarre to see how close the *favelas* were to the decadence of Copacabana, but I didn't really get it until I experienced it firsthand. I took out my camera and started snapping pictures, hoping one of my usual magazines would print them, so I could share the experience with the world.

When we arrived at the camp, we were met by a man who looked more like a college quarterback than a physician. He was tall and broad, and sported camouflage shorts, a T-shirt, and a shaved head.

"Clea Raymond," he said as we got out of the car. "Welcome to GloboReach. I'm Dr. Prichard." He pulled out his cell phone and added, "One moment."

One moment? I looked curiously at Ben.

"Hello ma'am, Dr. Prichard here," he said into the phone. "Yes, ma'am. She's here. . . . Yes, with her friend. . . . Yes, that's him. . . . You have my word. . . . Yes, of course."

He held the phone out to me. "Your mom."

Unbelievable. I took the phone. "Mom???"

"I know, you're not a child. I just want you to know you don't have to go through with this. If it's too hard, there's no shame in saying good-bye and going back to the hotel."

"Mom . . . I'm fine."

"I just worry, Clea."

I rolled my eyes. "I *want* to do this, Mom. Look, I promise if it's too hard I'll leave. Okay?"

"Okay. Good. I love you."

"Love you, too."

We clicked off, and I handed the phone back to Dr. Prichard, shaking off the mom moment. "Sorry about that," I said.

"No need. Want me to show you around?"

Dr. Prichard was all business. I could see how my dad would like him. He took us on the tour, and when we had seen the entire camp, he offered us seats outside his quarters. We sat, and I wiped my suddenly sweaty palms on my shorts. I'd been dying to have a conversation with this man for a year, but now that he was in front of me, it was hard to find the right way in. I decided to just go for it—he seemed like the kind of man who'd appreciate directness.

"So . . . what can you tell me about my dad's disappearance?"

Dr. Prichard nodded. He'd known this was coming. "I'm sorry, but I really don't have anything else to add to the story. It's exactly what I told everyone else: He left camp without telling anyone where he was going, the same way he did all the time. Only this time he didn't come back."

The words hung awkwardly between us. Then Dr. Prichard cleared his throat. "I'm sorry if that was too blunt. Your father was a good man. I respected him a great deal."

"No, it's fine. Thank you. I appreciate your honesty, and I know you've told the whole story before. It's just . . . if you could think about it . . . if there's anything else you can remember about the day he disappeared, anything at all, even if it seems completely insignificant . . . it would mean so much to me."

Dr. Prichard nodded again. He squinted into the sun, thinking it over. I kept quiet, giving him space. Finally he ran his hand over his scalp in a way that made me wonder if it was a gesture left over from the days before he'd shaved his head.

"Okay," he said, "I do have something. Just know that I do think it's completely insignificant."

"That's okay," I assured him. "I'd still love to hear it."

"We deal with a lot of heavy stuff at this camp," Dr. Prichard said. "One in five people who come to us has had a family member killed, and most of them have direct experience with violent acts. Seeing that again and again . . . it can wear you down. Your dad never let it. He always kept things light around here. He made jokes, he planned goofball things for us and the community—stupid stuff, like games of charades and obstacle courses—things to take our mind off the worst of it. But in the last few days before he disappeared, he wasn't like that. He was serious. Somber, even. Like he was wrestling with something."

"Do you know what it was?" I asked. "Was anything going on around camp? Maybe with a patient?"

"Not that I know of. My guess? A bad meal that tied his intestines in knots. Wouldn't be the first time that happened here. I told you, anything that mattered I've already said. But you asked, so . . ."

He got up. I guessed our conversation was done.

Ben and I rose as well. "Thank you," I said. "You have no idea how much I appreciate your time."

We all said our good-byes, then Ben and I climbed into the Jeep and started back to the hotel.

"It's interesting," Ben said, putting a voice to my thoughts, "but it doesn't really give us anything to go on."

"Maybe not," I agreed, but my mind was already racing. What could have changed Dad's mood? Had something gone wrong with a patient? Or maybe an ex-patient—someone outside the camp, so Dr. Prichard wouldn't have known. Maybe there was a family he tried to save from the drug trade. Could he have gotten too deeply involved, and had someone taken drastic steps to get him to butt out?

GloboReach technically belonged to our family now—I was sure I could find a way to get all Dad's files and go through them, see if any of his past patients or their families were involved in something shady that Dad might have gotten into.

Then again, didn't Dr. Prichard say nearly everyone they dealt with had experience with violent acts? There must be an endless list of Dad's ex-patients who could have inadvertently led him into something dangerous. The search could take forever, and I still might not find out anything for sure.

Ben leaned on the horn, and I snapped out of my reverie. We were caught behind a massive crowd of people dancing in the streets around a sound truck blaring samba music. Instinctively I stood in my seat for a better look, hooked my sunglasses over my shirt, and started snapping pictures.

"That's really not safe," Ben said.

"We're moving two miles an hour. I'll be okay."

And truthfully, the longer I lingered behind my camera, and the longer the samba music seeped into my system, the more I *felt* okay, and let everything else melt away. The whole scene in the streets was irresistible—the thrumming from the sound truck was enhanced by live drummers in feathered and beaded costumes. I didn't even realize I was moving my hips to the beat until Ben called me on it.

"How can you dance and take pictures at the same time?"

I laughed, and the sound unlocked the last bit of tension in my body. "Motion stabilization in the camera—can't live without it!"

Cruising slowly behind the revelers, our Jeep became part of the parade—even more so when two men wearing nothing but black thongs and bongos leaped aboard, screaming encouragement to the crowd.

"Seriously?" Ben groused. "No way. I'm going to get pulled over."

"How?" I shouted over the bongos. "The police are dancing too!"

I snapped a close-up of one of the bongo players, who then offered me a spot on his drum. We played together as Ben drove on, finally pulling into the hotel valet parking area, where the drummers leaped off the Jeep and ran ahead to continue with the crowd.

More music blared from inside the hotel. I felt it carry me, lighter than air. "Not so much for Carnival?" I asked Ben playfully, hooking my arm through his.

"Not so much for *driving* through Carnival," Ben amended.

"Too tough for you?"

"I travel with you. Nothing's too tough for me."

"Not even that guy?"

He turned to look, and the minute his attention was diverted, I raced to the elevators.

"Hey!" Ben cried, and ran after me, but I dove and pressed the button first.

"Yes!" I cheered.

"Loser," Ben said.

"Actually, I just won. Let's go up and change, then we can hit the Samba Parade."

"Change? But I like you just the way you are."

"You are such a dork."

Ben nodded, accepting the title with grace as the elevator arrived.

I'd thought we'd get ready and go back down right away, but once I got to my room, I realized how exhausted I was. I looked at the clock and was grateful to see we still had a few hours before we needed to get to the Sambadrome—enough time for a room service snack and a nap. I called Ben to tell him the new plan.

I didn't sleep that long, but it was enough to energize me. I woke up refreshed and excited for the Samba Parade. It was the perfect excuse to wear my favorite black sundress with the excellent twirling properties, and I felt light and breezy as I knocked on Ben's door. He swung it open and presented me with a single red rose.

"For you," he said.

"Very gallant," I replied. "Of course you do realize I have the same cut flower in my room."

Ben glanced over his shoulder at the now empty bud vase sitting on his table. "Hmm. Didn't really think that out. Still gallant?"

"Very."

"You happen to look ravishing tonight." He said it with a British accent that made me laugh out loud.

"As do you, sir," I responded in kind.

"Excellent. Shall we go, then?" He extended his arm and I linked my own through it, first shifting my camera bag to my other shoulder so it wouldn't bang between us.

Even upstairs we could hear the music from the streets, but it blared in our ears as the elevator doors opened. The hotel had its own Carnival party, and we wove through the crowd to the bar. Ben and I each ordered a drink, and they arrived in obscenely wide glasses overflowing with obnoxiously large cuts of tropical fruit.

"To Rio?" I giggled, offering my glass for a toast.

"To Rio," he replied.

We clinked glasses and drank, soaking in the atmosphere and the music until it felt like a crime to stay seated.

"Dance with me," I said.

"Clea," Ben said, balking, "you know I can't dance."

I did know that. And I also knew Ben didn't say no to me very often. I slipped off my bar stool and took both his hands, already sambaing as I carved out a path to the dance floor. It was crowded, but not painfully packed. Ben looked terrified. Clearly I was going to lead.

"Okay, what do I do here?" he asked.

I didn't answer. I just danced.

"What are you doing? I can't do that. It's impossible. My hips don't go like that. How do your hips go like that?" He tried moving with frenzied baby steps, completely out of rhythm with the music.

I put my hands on his hips. "Slow down. It's okay. Just relax, and let your hips go."

"I am relaxed. My hips are very shy; they don't like to go off without the rest of my body."

I laughed, and we danced through the end of the song, then took off for the Sambadrome, home of the official Samba Parade. The magazine that had hired me for the photo shoot had gotten us tickets in a *frisa*, or front box, as close to the parade runway as we could possibly get. We arrived about a half hour before the parade started, and the sound of the crowd was deafening. I clung to Ben's hand and my camera as we wormed our way through an endless sea of bodies to get to our seats. As a rule I hated crowds like this, but this place trumped that rule.

Fireworks exploded into the sky to start the parade, and the Queen of Carnival led the first group of dancers into the Sambadrome. I was in heaven. Ben looked pained.

"How much would you pay right now for earplugs?" I asked him. This was so not Ben's scene, but he was being great about it.

The parade transformed the street into a kaleidoscope of eye candy. Each group had hundreds of dancers and drummers, all in huge matching costumes with feathers, wings, mirrors, beads, bells, and more. They moved between massive floats that reached to the sky, and the floats themselves teemed with more dancers and musicians. It went on and on, with each group more over the top than the last. I wanted to look everywhere at once.

Ben and I stayed most of the night, dancing and taking pictures. By four in the morning the Sambadrome still raged, but part of my assignment was to cover things happening outside the Samba Parade, so we poured back into the city. It was more alive at this predawn hour than most cities at midday.

As the first shades of pink sunrise glowed in the sky, Ben and I made it to the beach by our hotel. Here, too, the party continued, with several lone drummers scattered along the sand, each one with a small group of people dancing around him. The atmosphere was charged but subdued—the final embers of an all-night celebration. Only one group seemed to still be going full steam—a crowd of what I pegged for frat guys who whooped and danced like the night had just begun. I snapped pictures of them and everything else happening on the beach, and then I was done. Work time was over.

I put my camera back in its case and breathed in the ocean air. My eyes were bleary, but I couldn't imagine going to sleep. Instead I turned to Ben.

"Dance with me," I said.

Amazingly, he did it without complaint, holding my hands and swaying to the beat of a nearby drummer. I kicked off my shoes to feel the sand on my toes, then closed my eyes, letting the music guide me. I let go of Ben and twirled around and around . . . until I lost my balance and fell. Ben caught me in his arms, then surprised me by spinning me into an expert dip.

I looked up. My whole field of vision was Ben. His face, so familiar, standing out against the early-morning sky. His rumpled brown hair, his nose just slightly too big for his face, his puppy-dog light brown eyes. A layer of thin stubble coated his chin, and I suddenly had the irresistible urge to touch it. I ran my fingers gently down his cheek. Scratchy.

"Clea." Ben's voice cracked a little on the word. He pulled me back upright, but he didn't let go. I didn't mind. I liked the feel of his arms around me. I remembered the night I came home from Europe, the way his damp tee clung to his chest. Without conscious effort, my eyes drifted down to the V of his blue button-down shirt, and for a wild second I imagined myself unbuttoning it, brushing my fingers against his skin as I did . . .

This was crazy. This was *Ben*. My friend.

I raised my eyes from his chest and looked at his face, but it was different from the face I'd always known. He looked serious, and sure of himself in a way I'd never seen. I liked it. He reached up his hand and pushed back my hair, tucking it behind my ear. Had he ever done that before? I didn't think so. It felt wonderful.

"Clea," he said again, softer this time. "There's something I want to tell you—"

"WHOOOOOOOO!!!!!!!"

It was a stampede of frat boys, the rowdy guys I'd snapped earlier. They stormed down the beach, and people leaped to get out of their way. Ben and

I tried to do the same, but we were split apart as the guys swarmed all around us and started dancing to our drummer.

"Ben?" I called. I couldn't even see him through the sea of bodies.

"Clea?"

He sounded pretty far away. I started snaking through the crowd to find him.

"Ben!"

"Clea!"

Better. He was closer now. I peered through gaps in the mass of bodies, straining to catch a glimpse of him . . .

. . . when suddenly I froze, and the entire world screeched to a stop.

The man from my dreams was with us on the beach.

SIX

"CLEA!" BEN CRIED as he burst through the crowd to stand in front of me.

I didn't even see him. My eyes were locked fifty feet down the beach, where the man stood alone, scanning the sand with a furrowed brow, as if searching for something he'd lost.

He wore jeans, a leather jacket, and a gray T-shirt.

Suddenly he lifted his head and looked right at me. It was the face I knew as well as I knew my own, and I watched as his eyes filled with a shock that exactly mirrored mine.

Then he turned away and fled down the beach.

"NO!" I shouted, and immediately took off after him.

"Clea?" Ben called, but I barely even heard him. I was focused only on the man. I couldn't let him get away. I strained to catch up before he flew out of sight.

The man was fast, but so was I. I could easily clock a six-minute mile on the treadmill, and Krav Maga kept my endurance high. I chased him all the way across Copacabana Beach, dodging and darting around scattered knots of partiers.

When he reached Leme Hill, the jungly mountain at the northernmost end of the beach, the man didn't stop. He plunged forward, eschewing the cleared dirt trail for the camouflage of the overgrown brush. I followed without hesitation, despite the fact that I'd left my shoes far behind. He had the advantage now, and I quickly lost sight of him, but he left a trail of trampled plants, and I plowed after him, my breath rasping in my throat as I pushed my legs harder and faster.

I never saw the knot of roots. One minute I was running my hardest, the next I was screaming at a searing pain in my ankle and landing face-first in the brush.

"NO!!!" I screamed, far more frustrated over losing him than any injury I might have. I tried to get up, but my left ankle wouldn't take my weight, and I thumped back onto the ground.

"Shit!" I winced, shifting to examine my rapidly swelling ankle. "Shit-shit-shit-SHIT!"

I tried to stand again, gingerly this time, but my ankle wouldn't have it, and I plopped back down.

Great. I was all by myself in the middle of nowhere with a ripped-up ankle, completely unable to move. Defeat rushed over me like an avalanche, and I suddenly felt the impact of it all: my dad, the nightmares, the dreams, the secrets, the pain, and oh my God I was so, so tired. I just wanted to be six years old and curled up in bed with my mommy and daddy tucking me in and kissing me good night.

That was what I wanted. It was so simple and yet so completely and hopelessly impossible. With nothing left to hang on to, I curled into myself and sobbed uncontrollably.

"Hey . . . you okay?"

I recognized the voice—how had my dreams known his voice?—but when he crouched down next to me, I skittered away.

"Don't touch me!" I snapped.

He held up his hands to show he was harmless. "Okay, okay," he said with a smirk. "You were the one chasing me."

I glared at him. It was an impressive show of restraint on my part, when the truth was that having him physically in front of me was wreaking havoc on my body and my brain. My heart was pounding fast, and my mind played a loop of every moment we'd shared in my dreams.

I forced myself to remember he was a stranger. Quite possibly a dangerous stranger. I needed answers from him, but I also needed to stay strong.

"I'm sorry," he said. "I thought you were hurt."

"I *am* hurt. I twisted my ankle."

"Maybe you shouldn't be chasing strange men through the woods, then."

"Maybe you shouldn't pretend you don't know who I am."

His eyes widened in shock for a moment. "You reme—"

Then he twitched his head briefly to the side, as if flicking away an unwanted thought, and his face relaxed. Only the clenched muscle in his jaw gave away any tension.

"You must be mistaken. I don't think we've ever met."

"Really? You look at most girls like you were caught with your hand in their purse?"

"I don't know what you're talking—"

"And then you ran away. Full speed, even though you knew I was trying to catch up with you. That's not normal. That's not how you act with a stranger."

The man pursed his lips and pressed his right fist to his temple, a gesture I'd seen him make so many times I almost lost my grip. Somehow I managed to stay steely eyed.

He lowered his fist and smiled, though the smile didn't reach his eyes.

"I reacted poorly," he said stiffly. "I don't have a good answer for why, other than I like to keep to myself. I only came back because you were hurt, and it seemed irresponsible to leave a girl all alone in the middle of nowhere. But if you'd rather I left . . ."

"No."

"Fine. Let's take a look at your ankle."

He crouched down and raised his eyebrows, asking for my leg. I stretched it out toward him, and as he took it in his hands, there was a crashing sound in the foliage behind us.

"Oh my God, get away from her! What did you do?"

I wheeled to see a red-faced Ben leap into the clearing and shove the man back.

"Ben!" I objected.

"Easy," the man said, rising. "She's hurt. I'm just looking at—"

"Get. Away. From. Her," Ben growled.

"Ben, stop," I said.

He looked at me, confused, then turned back to the man. His whole body leaned forward, like a pit bull straining against its leash. In another situation it might be funny: lanky, bookish Ben even dreaming he could pose a threat to this brick wall of a man.

The man backed away. "It's not broken or sprained," he said, nodding toward my ankle. "It's just a strain. She should be fine by tomorrow."

Ben kept his eyes on the man, but he spoke to me, his voice calm and studied. "What you need to do is simple, Clea. Tell him he doesn't affect you. Command him to leave you and never come back. Say you compel him to go forth and wander the world forever on foot."

Had he lost his mind? "What are you talking about?"

"Ancient mythology," Ben said. "It's how you get rid of an incubus."

"A what?" The man laughed.

Ben wasn't amused. "Do it, Clea."

"Please . . . don't bother," the man said, holding up his hands. "I'll get out of your way."

He made a move for the woods, and I was about to scream "NO!" at the top of my lungs, but I didn't have to.

"STOP!" Ben leaped for the man, his muscles taut with rage. He grabbed the man's wrist and held it in front of his face. "Where did you get this?"

My eyes grew wide as I realized what Ben had found. I couldn't believe I hadn't noticed it myself. On anyone else I would have, but seeing this man in the flesh had my head spinning with so many other things. . . .

The man was wearing my dad's watch. A silver Omega. He and my mom had bought each other matching ones the first day of their honeymoon, and they rarely took them off. On the rare occasions when one of them thought they'd lost their watch, the world stopped, and we had to drop everything and turn the house upside down until we found it.

That watch was on the man's wrist.

"I don't know what you're talking about," he said. "It's just my watch."

"Bullshit." Ben unclasped the watch and pulled it over the man's hand, then tossed it to me. "Clea?"

My hands shook as I inspected the watch. It was true, there were many watches out there that looked just liked my dad's. It wasn't impossible that this man would have the same make and model.

Then I turned the watch over to look at the back of the casing. Engraved in fine italic print were the words GRANT—YOU HAVE ALL MY LOVE FOREVER. VICTORIA.

There were some scratches below the engraving, but that didn't matter. The watch was without question my father's.

My whole body was trembling now. I felt sick fury boiling inside me even as I struggled against tears. "What did you do to him?!" I screamed.

"Nothing," the man objected. "I did nothing. You're right. The watch isn't mine. A man gave it to me."

"Liar," Ben snarled.

Clutching the watch in my hand, I struggled to my feet. My ankle was still too sore to use, so I hopped the few steps to Ben and leaned on him. I stared into the man's eyes and blocked out everything except what I knew for sure: He was connected to my father. My eyes bored into his, and I hissed through the pain in my ankle, "That watch is my father's. He would never give it to anyone. Never. I need you to tell me who the hell you are and how the hell you got his watch."

The man raised an eyebrow, and I realized there was something patently absurd about me trying to strong-arm him when I couldn't even hold myself upright without help.

The man held up the wrist that Ben still squeezed in a death grip. "Can I have my arm back first?"

"What, so you can run away?" Ben snapped. "Do you think I'm stupid?"

The man just looked at him. "If I really wanted to run, neither one of you could stop me."

He was right, of course. "Let him go," I said.

"Clea . . ."

"I want to hear what he has to say. Let him go."

Ben released the man's arm.

I took a second to tuck my father's watch safely inside my camera bag, then fixed the man with a stare and asked, "Who are you?"

He took a deep breath, as if the answer required a long story, but then he let it out and replied simply, "I'm Sage. It's nice to meet you, Clea."

Sage. I felt a thrill when I heard him say my name.

"Nice necklace," Sage added.

"What the hell?" Ben exploded. "This isn't a cocktail party!"

"Your boyfriend's very protective," Sage said. "That's good."

"I'm not interested in what you think," I said.

That was such a lie. I was very interested in what he thought, and I desperately wanted him to know that Ben was not my boyfriend. I tried to ignore the feeling.

"Grant Raymond, my father, disappeared over a year ago, from right around here. You have his watch. Can you explain that?"

Sage ignored my question. "Your father was a good man," he said. "Be safe, Clea. Live a long, happy life."

He reached out and grazed his fingers over my cheek. My skin tingled at his touch. I leaned in for more, but he was gone, already pushing through the brush.

"WAIT!" I was furious at my body for betraying me so I couldn't run after him. I'd finally found Sage. I knew without a doubt that he was the man from my dreams. Not just someone who looked like him. It was *him*—the one who saw me like no one else ever had—and now I could only watch him disappear into the woods. I still had no idea how he knew my father. Had Sage hurt him? I didn't think so, but my head was spinning with so many different feelings, I didn't know what to believe.

Ben pulled out his cell phone.

"He's not gonna get away. I'm calling the police. I'm gonna tell them he's involved with your dad's disappearance. We can describe him—we even have pictures. Wait—no—we can't show them the pictures, that would get too complicated. Do you think we should show them the pictures?"

I heard Ben's manic voice, but I had no idea what he was saying. I couldn't take my eyes off the last spot in the brush where I'd seen Sage.

Thump! A huge black blob fell from the trees and landed on Ben, pinning him to the ground.

"BEN!"

Before I could move, someone else grabbed my arms, pinning them behind my back. Automatically I kicked my good heel back as hard as possible, nailing my assailant in the groin. His arms loosened, and I shot my elbow backward into his face, then wheeled and drove jab after jab into his solar plexus . . . until another person grabbed my arms from behind and lifted me into the air. I flailed and kicked, then the first guy grabbed my legs and pinned them to his sides.

"Ooh, we got ourselves a feisty one!" The man's accent was European, thick and difficult to understand. I threw my head back to see his face; I wanted to give a good description when I got the chance. I smelled it before I could see it: the stench of decay from his black, ruined teeth. His pasty cheeks were sunken. Open sores stood out on his forehead and chin. He had a huge, faded tattoo across his throat: a skull with fire bursting out of its eye sockets and the letters CV below it. He looked sickly, but he was strong. I couldn't move my arms.

His face spread in a wide, reeking smile. "Hey! Look who it is!" He turned to his friends—the one securing my legs, and the one who was holding Ben. "Look who we've got! It's that woman's daughter. It's . . . what's her name? Clea! Clea Raymond! We got a celebrity on our hands. A rich celebrity. Just think about the possibilities, gentlem—"

Whoosh! Something swung down from the trees and slammed him violently on the bridge of his nose, which exploded in blood. As the man lost consciousness he dropped my arms, and my body swung downward. My head smashed hard onto the ground. I literally saw stars. I fought really hard to shake them off. The world grew more and more distant and fuzzy . . . until it faded out.

The world started to come back well before I could open my eyes.

I couldn't see yet, but I could feel.

It felt like I was moving.

Quickly. I was moving very quickly.

I was moving very quickly, but I wasn't doing the work. How was that possible?

Wait—I felt arms clutching my legs.

It was the guy—it had to be—the one who'd had my legs. He still had them, and now I was . . . yes, I was slung over his shoulder and he was running with me.

As my senses continued to return, I tried to work out an advantage. Did I have one? Was there a way out?

I did have one advantage: The guy holding me had to think I was still unconscious. I felt for his shirt and jacket, and carefully pulled them up.

I took a deep breath, then as hard and as fast as I could, I dug my nails into his skin, feeling the satisfaction of four long channels of blood opening in their wake.

"OW!!" the man screamed.

My eyes flew open, and in a flash all my senses returned. That voice. It was Sage.

I was slung over *Sage's* shoulder, and he was running.

Was he kidnapping me?

I could move now, and I writhed and flailed against him. "Put me down!"

"Stop it!" Sage growled, and behind me Ben's voice hissed, "Clea!"

I looked up and saw Ben. He put his fingers to his lips, then pointed behind him.

It all came together now. Sage had saved us, but we were still in trouble. I probably hadn't been unconscious that long; we were still in the same junglelike brush as before.

Suddenly a rush of panic surged through me.

"My camera!" I hissed to Ben. My camera bag wasn't on my shoulder. My father's watch was inside. I'd lost it.

Ben held up the camera bag. Of course he wouldn't leave it behind. I could have kissed him.

So we were safe for the moment . . . safe-ish . . . but I still didn't like being helplessly slung over someone's shoulder. I almost demanded that Sage let me down again, but between my throbbing head and unsteady ankle, we'd probably move faster if I stayed where I was.

My head was still a little swimmy, and something was nagging at me. Something the attackers had said . . . but I couldn't put my finger on it. It didn't help that I probably had a concussion, and was now hanging upside down and bouncing around. Holding my head up was making me nauseous, so I hung back down. Also not comfortable. I thought about Rayna, how she swore by her yoga classes and the way they "allowed her body to achieve maximum relaxation." I wondered if she'd be able to find a position that was comfortable while jouncing around inverted on someone's back. I wondered if she'd be more or less relaxed in this position if she knew the back in question belonged to a possible incubus who'd been haunting her dreams.

I giggled.

I was clearly not one hundred percent.

"In here," I heard Sage whisper, and he slung me off his shoulder and into his arms. He was standing in front of what looked like solid brush, but he parted the foliage with his foot to reveal a small hole. Ben crawled inside. Then Sage looked down at me.

"You okay to crawl?" he whispered.

I nodded, and he set me down on the ground. I had to lower myself almost completely flat to get inside, and I clawed my way forward for what seemed like an eternity. I couldn't see a thing, but I could hear the scratch of Ben's shoes just ahead of me. I listened for Sage behind me. I couldn't hear him. Was he there? I didn't even have room to turn around in here.

My throat grew tight and I couldn't swallow. What if this was a trap? What if Sage *was* an evil spirit, and this was how he'd strike? What if Ben was about to reach a dead end? We'd try to crawl backward . . . only to find that Sage had closed off the entrance, leaving us to suffocate in this makeshift coffin.

Was that how he got my dad's watch? Had Sage killed my father?

I started hyperventilating, but forced in a slow, long breath, willing calm into my body. Losing consciousness now would be the worst thing I could do. I was letting myself go back to Extreme Thinking, when I had to be in the moment and aware. Like Rayna doing her yoga.

Rayna. Yoga. Aware.

I recited it like a mantra to help me stay calm, and within moments the crawlway opened into a large cave, with ceilings eight feet high. A tiny bit of light streamed in from above, just enough to make out the space and Ben. He rushed over to help me to my feet.

"Tell me I'm not the only one who thought he'd set us up," he murmured.

"Totally imagined a huge dead end," I agreed.

We laughed with giddy relief as Sage emerged into the cave.

"Are you okay?" he asked.

I nodded, and then I remembered—the thing that had been nagging me.

"The men who attacked us . . . they didn't know who I was at first."

"Because they weren't after you," Sage said. "They're after me."

"Who's after you?" I asked. "Why?"

"I can't tell you that."

"You should," I countered. "If you don't, I could turn you in as the guy behind my father's disappearance."

Sage looked at me in disbelief. "I just saved your life. Doesn't that mean anything?"

"Not if you won't admit what you know. You could be just as dangerous as they are."

"You really believe that?"

He looked at me, and we both knew I didn't believe it at all. Not really. But I wasn't going to admit it. I held his gaze as he leaned against the wall and lowered himself to the ground, settling in.

"Fine," he said. "I'll tell you everything I can. I have to, because as things stand now . . . we're stuck together."

seven

"ACTUALLY," Ben countered, "we're not stuck together at all. We're staying here only until we're safe. Then we leave, and if you're lucky, we don't turn you in to the police."

"That's funny," Sage said, then turned to me. "Your boyfriend's funny. But you're not going to the police when we get out of here, because the last thing you want is for me to be anywhere except by your side."

"Yeah, right," Ben scoffed.

"Listen, I know how these guys work. They saw me help you, so now they think we're together and they can use you to get to me. I've seen it happen before." Sage turned to me, and his face grew serious. "I saw it happen with your father."

"You need to tell me how you know him," I said. "I want to know everything. Where did you meet him?"

"I didn't, really. He met me. He came looking for me because I have information about something he was interested in."

"Which was . . .?" I urged.

Sage took a deep breath, then let it out as he replied, "Something called the Elixir of Life."

Ben perked up. "What do you know about the Elixir of Life?"

"*I* know it's ridiculous! Please tell me my dad wasn't taken by some psychopath who thought it was real."

"I can't tell you that," Sage said.

"But that's so stupid!" The waste of it was more than I could handle. The idea that someone could hurt my dad because of something that didn't even exist . . .

"Grant didn't think it was stupid," Ben said, cutting into my thoughts. "He believed in it. He knew it would be the ultimate breakthrough in modern medicine."

"It's not medicine," I said. "It's a fairy-tale drink that makes people live forever."

"In large doses," Ben said. "In smaller doses it has incredible healing powers. It cures any disease."

"Are you listening to yourself?" I asked.

"You haven't seen all your dad's research. He has volumes of it, and it's not just myths, it's in history, too. How do you think he knew where to dig up the vials?"

"The *empty* vials," I clarified.

"Empty," Sage chimed in, "because the Elixir had been moved somewhere else. That's the information I have—I know where it is."

"You know where it is?" Ben's entire energy changed; suddenly his whole face filled with excitement.

"I do." Sage spoke slowly, as if it were an effort to make sure he chose just the right words. "But I don't know exactly how to get it. It's like I have only one piece of the puzzle. Clea's father said he had the rest."

Ben nodded eagerly. "Okay, wow, this totally makes sense . . . but how did he know where to find you?"

"I don't know," Sage said. "I didn't make it

easy. I've been in hiding from two very dangerous groups of people who would do anything to get the Elixir: the Saviors of Eternal Life and Cursed Vengeance."

"Cursed Vengeance," I murmured. "CV. The guy who grabbed me had 'CV' tattooed on his neck."

"So that was them," Sage agreed. "Both groups have been around a long time, but they seemed to get stronger after your father excavated the Elixir vials, so I made myself disappear. No one had ever found me until he knocked on my door. It was shocking, actually, and I never would have let him in except I recognized him from all the news stories. Plus, he looked so serious. . . ."

"Like Dr. Prichard said," I realized. "He told us Dad was very intense the days before he disappeared."

"That's right," Ben agreed. Then he thought of something, and his jaw dropped. "Whoa—what about when he saw you? Seeing you in person for the first time after so many years . . ."

"He acted very strange," Sage admitted. "But . . . what do you mean 'so many years'?"

"The pictures," I said. "You've been showing up in my pictures all my life."

"I have?" Sage looked at me wonderingly. "That's very odd . . . because I've never seen you before today."

I don't know what I expected him to say, but it wasn't that. I thought he'd be the one person who could explain the pictures. If he was as confused by them as I was, what did that mean? I stared into his eyes—was he lying? No—he looked genuinely amazed. I had no idea what to say, so I reached for something real.

"What happened next with my dad?" I asked.

"He said he knew how to help me retrieve the Elixir, and that we needed to speak to a 'dark lady.'"

"A 'dark lady'?" I asked dubiously. "That's not how my dad would speak."

"That's what he said," Sage maintained.

"Did he say where you'd find her?" Ben asked.

"No," Sage said. "He just promised to take me to her. We made arrangements to meet the next day, in the Tijuca Forest."

He turned to me. "I think your dad was afraid I wouldn't show. He gave me his watch as a strange kind of reverse collateral. He said it was his most prized possession. He said he knew I was a good person, and I wouldn't run off with something that meant so much to him."

I smiled. That was my dad's way: He always believed people lived up or down to the amount of trust you put in them.

"What happened? What went wrong?" Ben asked. "Why didn't you guys go?"

"I don't know," Sage admitted. "He never showed. I thought maybe something had come up, so I went to the same spot at the same time the next day. And the next. For several days. Then I saw on the news that he'd disappeared, and I knew it wasn't safe for me here anymore. I left the country."

"That's it?" I snapped. "You didn't go to the police? You didn't go to . . . oh, maybe *my family*?"

"I couldn't put myself out there like that," Sage said defensively. "I couldn't have the attention."

"How dare you? We're talking about my dad's life! If you'd told us about these groups, we could have spent the last year going after them! He could be alive right now!"

"You're assuming he's not," Sage said.

I opened my mouth to retort, then snapped it shut as I realized the import of his words.

"You think my father's still alive?"

"I think it's very likely. To get the Elixir, either group needs both what Grant knows and what I know. Unless Grant was foolish enough to give them his information, he's still alive."

"Wait," Ben said. "If whichever group needed you both, why did they just kidnap him? Why didn't they wait until you were together in the forest?"

"Grant must have realized they were following him, so he changed the plans. He probably thought it would keep us both safe, but instead they decided to strike and at least get him. As you saw this morning . . . they're still after me."

"So you think he's alive." I almost hated to think it. I wanted it so badly. The idea that my dad could actually be alive—even if he was hurt, even if he'd been tortured . . . it felt like too much to hope for.

"So what do we do?" I asked. "How can we find my father?"

"And the Elixir of Life," Ben added.

"There *is* no Elixir of Life," I said.

"Yes, there is," Ben and Sage chorused.

"No, there isn't. And even if there were, I wouldn't care unless it helped me find my father."

"Which it might," Sage said.

Ben and I both wheeled to face him.

"How?" I asked.

"We take the trip I was supposed to take with Grant. We find the dark lady. She'll help us get the Elixir. That's what whoever has your father wants.

We get that, we have the ultimate bargaining chip."

"But we don't know who or where this lady is," Ben said.

"Dad would have figured it out before he came down here to tell Sage, right?" I said. "That means he worked on it at home. You know how he wrote everything down and kept all his research. I bet somewhere in the house there's some kind of information about what he had planned."

Ben turned to Sage. "Okay. So all Clea and I need is for you to tell us what you know about the Elixir, and we can go get it. You won't ever have to see us again."

"Not possible," Sage said. "I said it before; you've been tied to me. That means you're in danger. I don't think you get that."

"Oh, I get it," Ben said, "I just think Clea and I will be safer on our own. And with all due respect, I don't entirely trust you. And I don't think Clea does either."

"Respect duly noted," Sage said wryly, "but I'm not telling you what I know about the Elixir, so you kind of need me."

The two guys stared each other down.

"Fine," I jumped in, "so we'll all go to Connecticut together."

"You say that like it's simple," Sage said. "You don't think whoever has your father—or anyone looking for the Elixir—has their eye on your house? I'd be surprised if it hadn't been searched for clues regularly since Grant first found the vials. Now that you're involved too, the place will probably be crawling with people"

"Impossible. No one could get past security at my house."

But even as I said it, I thought about my dad's office, and my certainty that someone had gone through it. I caught Ben's eye and he nodded, remembering the same thing.

"Okay," I said to Sage. "How do we find what we need if it's in the house, then?"

"We go there, but we're smart about it. I need you both to listen to me. I'd say 'trust me,' but that might be too much to ask."

Ben crossed his arms over his chest. I looked at Sage noncommittally.

"Right," Sage noted. "We have to fly completely under the radar. Either of you ever done that before?"

I shook my head.

"The first thing we do is wait until night. My guess is those guys are long gone by now, but I'd rather play it safe. It will also give your ankle a chance to heal. I'd carry you," he added, "but I'd have to get you declawed first."

"Don't count on it," I replied.

Sage did an exaggerated stretch. "In the meantime, I think we should all get some sleep." He sprawled out across the dirt floor. "Good night."

He shut his eyes and was perfectly still. There was no chance he was asleep already, but Ben spoke his mind anyway. He pulled me aside just the slightest bit and sneered down at Sage.

"I don't like any of this, Clea."

"Really? Because when he started talking about the Elixir of Life, I thought the two of you were ready to become blood brothers."

"I believe in the Elixir," Ben said. "Enough that I want to believe Sage's story. I just don't know if we can. And we still can't explain the pictures. I don't trust him."

"I don't care, Ben. *Dad* trusted him. And Sage's plan is my best shot at finding him alive."

"I guess. Just . . ." Ben took a moment to put together his next words. "Be careful around him, okay? I feel like . . ."

I waited, but he wasn't going to finish. "Feel like what?"

"Nothing. I'm here for you. You know that, right?"

I could see him struggling. It was like he was trying to tell me something monumental, but the words that came out weren't doing it justice.

He sprawled out on the cave floor as far away from Sage as he could, and patted his chest. "Need a pillow? It's not really in my job description, but I'm happy to offer." He pinched a corner of his shirt between two fingers. "Cotton twill. Very soft."

I forced a laugh. "I'm okay. Thanks."

I curled up on the cave floor in between the two guys. Despite everything, I could already feel myself drifting away.

"Clea?" It was Ben's voice, now right next to my ear, but I was too tired to turn and respond. I think I managed a "Hmm?" but that might have been in my head.

"Good night," he said, then I heard him lie back down.

Sleeping on the cold hard earth is underrated—at least when you're really tired. I was actually very comfortable, and had no doubt I'd be asleep in no time.

I could only imagine what my dreams would hold.

eight

I WAS OLIVIA, and I sat in a rowboat oared by Sage along the Tiber River.

"If you think the Society is so ridiculous, tell your father you refuse to go!" I said.

"Really? And lose my share of the family fortune? I'd be destitute. You'd have to leave me for a Medici—a fiancé who could keep you in the style to which you're accustomed."

"Paints, canvas, and you. That's all I need. Maybe a little extra artistic talent."

Sage gave me a pointed look. He loved my artwork and always gave me a hard time for doubting my own ability. I liked to remind him he was biased.

"How about food?" he asked. "You'd need food."

"Wild fruits and vegetables."

"Roof over your head?"

"We'll build a hut."

"Clothing?"

I gave Sage a knowing smile, and he almost tipped the boat.

"Sage!" I cried, holding the sides for dear life. "I can't swim!"

"I'm sorry, but that was an absolutely valid response. Any man would tell you the same."

I laughed. "So what do you do in the Society meetings?"

"I can't tell you. I'm sworn to absolute secrecy." He said it with a haughty affectation that I mimicked as I pretended to zip closed my lips and throw away the key.

"My lips are sealed," I intoned.

"Really? Because mine are not."

He deftly pulled his oars into the boat so he could sit across from me and bend his head to mine as he spilled, exaggerating every word and gesture to make the story larger than life.

"The Society, my love, is a circle of far-too-wealthy men and women — myself included, thank God — who have clearly gotten so bored counting their money that they have to make up fairy-tale rituals to keep life interesting. Their specific fairy tale of choice . . ." Sage looked over his right, then his left shoulder, pretending to make sure no one was eavesdropping, then said in a loud stage whisper, *"The Elixir of Life!"*

"The what?!"

"Exactly."

"What does it do?"

"Let's see . . . it's an *elixir* . . . and it grants eternal *life* . . ."

"You're making fun of me."

"Only a little."

"Tell me more," I said. "Does it work?"

"What do you think?"

"Has anyone in the Society ever died?" I asked. "That would be the proof in the pudding, wouldn't it? Or in the Elixir."

"It would. And the answer is yes. They drop off as easily as anyone."

"Doesn't that put an end to the argument?"

"To me, yes," Sage said. "To the believers, no. They'd say using the Elixir to save lives is outside the natural order. It should only be used in the tiniest amounts to relieve pain and suffering as someone is on their way out."

"So they have the power to grant eternal life and they never use it? Seems like a waste."

"A waste of *time*! Each meeting is three hours long! Do you have any idea what I could do with three hours, Olivia?"

He had set me up for it that time, and I took the bait. "I can think of a few things you could do," I said, giving him another wicked smile. This time he returned the grin and leaned in close to kiss me, first on my lips, then my cheek, my neck. . . .

"Sage," I murmured as we slid down to the floor of the boat. "I really can't swim."

"Hmmm," he breathed into my ear, "then we'll just have to be very careful, won't we?"

I woke to the sound of light scratching, and for a long time I was positive it was something scraping along the bottom of the boat. Little by little I remembered myself. I wasn't in a boat, I was in a cave. I wasn't Olivia, I was Clea.

But I was with Sage.

My body was still heavy with sleep, so I didn't move, just opened my eyes.

The quality of light coming into the cave was subdued now. Moonlight.

Sage crouched on the ground, leaning over the cave floor a few feet in front of me. He held a small rock and concentrated on scratching something into the dirt. I could see the tension in his arms as he worked, and the small concentrated furrow between his brows. The moonlight cast a glowing aura on his skin. He was beautiful.

Whatever else he was, Sage was by far the most magnetic man I had ever seen. I had felt it in my dreams, and it was even more true in real life. I welcomed the chance to study him without his knowledge.

He glanced up, and I quickly closed my eyes, feigning sleep. Had he seen me? The scratching stopped. He was looking at me, I knew it. I held my breath and willed my eyes not to pop open and see if he was staring.

Finally the scratching started up again. I forced myself to slowly count to ten before I opened my eyelids the tiniest bit and peeked through my lashes.

Good—he wasn't looking at me.

I opened my eyes a little wider. What was he doing? Moving only my eyes, I glanced down at the dirt floor in front of him . . .

. . . and saw a picture of me, fast asleep.

It was incredible. I could see his tools laid out beside the picture: rocks in several sizes and shapes, a couple of twigs . . . the most rudimentary materials, and yet what he was etching into the floor wouldn't look out of place on an art gallery wall. It was beautiful . . . far more beautiful than I thought I actually looked in my sleep. Is that how he saw me?

Sage lifted his head again, and I shut my eyes. I imagined him studying me, taking careful note of my features and filtering them through his own senses. My heartbeat quickened, and it took all my willpower to remain still.

"You can keep pretending to be asleep if you'd like, but I don't see a career for you as an actress," he teased.

My eyes sprang open. Sage's head was again bent over his etching, but a grin played on his face as he worked.

"You knew?" I asked, mortified.

Sage put a finger to his lips, glancing toward Ben. "About two minutes before you woke up, I knew," he whispered. "Your breathing changed." He bent back over the drawing, then impishly asked, "Pleasant dreams?"

My heart stopped, and I felt myself blush bright crimson as I remembered our encounter in the bottom of the rowboat. I sent a quick prayer to whoever or whatever might be listening that I hadn't re-enacted any of it in my sleep, then said as nonchalantly as possible, "I don't know, I can't remember what I dreamed about. Why?"

He swapped out the rock in his hand for one with a thinner edge and worked for another moment. "No reason . . . just heard my name."

I hoped the dim moonlight shadowed the worst of my blush. "Your name," I reiterated. "That's . . . interesting. They say dreams sort out things that happen when we're awake."

"Hmm. Did you sort anything out?" he asked.

"Like I said, I can't remember."

I knew he didn't believe me. Time to change the subject. I nodded to the etching. "Can I come look?"

He sat back on his heels and gestured to his artwork. "By all means. I'm done."

I got up, happily noting that my ankle was now pain free. I carefully tiptoed around the two square feet of floor over which his drawing sprawled, and settled in next to him. "It's beautiful," I told him. "I'm flattered. I've never had anyone draw a picture of me before."

Sage cocked his head and studied what he'd etched. "You think it looks like you?"

Again a hot crawl of embarrassment raced up my neck and flooded my face. I looked more closely at the etching. The image did look like me, but only if you really wanted to see the resemblance. The woman in it had the same hair, and slept in the same position I had, but on closer inspection her features were quite different. Her eyes were farther apart, her nose more pointed, her cheekbones less defined . . . differences that seemed insignificant when I'd assumed the picture was of me, but knowing it wasn't . . .

I was an egocentric idiot. My dreams about this man may have been vivid, but they were *dreams*. They had nothing to with reality; not mine, and clearly not his. I stammered, groping for some kind of explanation. I had nothing.

"She does look like you, a little," Sage admitted. His eyes lingered on the contours of the drawing's face. I was eager to change the subject, but I felt like I had to ask.

"Who is she?"

"Someone I loved a long time ago," he murmured.

I suddenly felt an overwhelming need to comfort him and take away his pain, but I didn't know how. Then I thought of something.

"Let me look at your back," I said.

"My back?"

"Your scratches. I dug in pretty deep. I should make sure it's not infected."

"No, no, it's not," he said, waving me off. "It's fine."

"Just let me look."

Sage shook his head. "We're in a cave. It's not like you can clean it anyway."

Why was he being so difficult? I started to get frustrated. "Are you kidding me? You've asked me to believe the most ridiculous things I've ever heard. All I'm asking is for you to show me your stupid scratches!"

Sage rolled his eyes. "Fine," he said, and turned, lifting up his jacket and shirt.

That was weird.

The scratches were gone.

Completely gone. There wasn't even a mark.

But I'd dug in deep enough to make him bleed, hadn't I?

I shook my head—I must have been swimmy from the fall and remembered it wrong. Nobody healed that completely that fast.

I gasped as I remembered someone who did—Sage himself. In my dream. When I was Anneline and he cut his hand on the rose thorns.

"What is it, Doctor?" Sage asked. "Gangrene set in?"

Should I tell him about the dreams? I opened my mouth to do it. . . .

"Got an itch?" Ben asked. There was a harsh edge to his voice, and both Sage and I swung around to see him glaring at us. I felt caught, even though I wasn't doing anything wrong. Sage didn't seem bothered.

"Good morning, sleepyhead," Sage said.

Ben ignored him. He looked down at the drawing on the floor.

"Nice picture," he said. "Doesn't do her justice."

Sage didn't bother to correct him about the picture's subject. "It's dark. Let's move. Ankle all better?" he asked me.

I rotated my foot. There was a twinge of pain, but not a lot. "I'm good."

"Great."

He led us to a small tunnel at the far end of the cave. This was a much larger passageway than the crawl space through which we had entered, and it soon fed us back out into the brush of Leme Hill.

It was late at night, but the sky was bright and clear, aglow with the full moon and an unfathomable number of stars.

The minute we were out of the cave, my cell phone went crazy. "Rayna," I said, checking the screen. "She called six times. And she texted six more. She must be freaking out that we haven't checked in."

Before I could call her back, Sage snatched the phone away and flung it far into the woods.

"What are you doing?"

"Saving us from being tracked. Remember what I said about going below the radar? No cell phones, no credit cards, no ATM cards." Sage looked pointedly at Ben, but he shook his head.

"My cell's already gone," he said. "I lost it when we were jumped."

"Good. That's good. Let's go." We took a small path through the woods. Even though Sage believed the attackers were long gone, I kept jumping at every twig that cracked. I was grateful when we emerged onto the beach and walked back to the street. It was much quieter this Ash Wednesday night than it had been the night before, but it felt safer to be out in public.

Sage hailed a cab and climbed up front. Ben and I took the back.

"I don't like this, Clea," Ben said quietly. "This is textbook Bad Idea. We're driving with a stranger, no one knows where we are, and we have no way of getting in touch with anyone. This is exactly how people become statistics."

"Exactly?" I asked, thinking of all the bizarre twists and turns that had led us to this place.

Ben ceded the point with a sideways shrug. "Maybe not *exactly*. But still . . ."

He let it go, and the cab eventually stopped at the edge of a remote, forested area. Sage got out and paid. "Everybody out!"

Ben looked at me, one eyebrow raised. He was leaving the choice to me. I gave his knee a quick squeeze before I opened the door and we piled out of the car.

Sage waited for the cab to drive away, then ducked onto a forest path, clearly assuming we'd follow.

The path through the thick foliage was stunning in the moonlight, and I automatically released my camera from its bag.

"I wish you wouldn't," Sage said without turning around. "You know I'm not one for visitors."

"I'll refrain from selling the pictures to *Travel and Leisure,* then," I said, already snapping away. "Besides, I need something to take my mind off my feet." My shoes were still on the beach, where I'd kicked them off to dance.

"Hey, I offered to carry you," Sage offered.

"No, thank you."

I suppose I should have been able to move swiftly and silently without my shoes, but I only managed to stab myself on something with every other footfall, giving me a sideways, hopping gait. Every few minutes Sage would hold out his arms, offering to carry me again. I grimaced and denied him each time.

After what felt like about ten miles, even the photos weren't distracting enough. "How much farther?" I asked.

"We're here."

There was nothing in front of us but more trees.

"Wow," Ben said, and I followed his eyes upward to see that several of the tree trunks were actually stilts supporting a beautifully hidden wood-and-glass cabin, set high among the branches. I was immediately charmed.

"You live in a tree house," I said. I aimed my camera at the facade, answering Sage's objection before he even said it. "For me, not for *Architectural Digest*."

"Thank you," Sage said.

We followed him up the stairs and went inside. The cabin wasn't large—the sloping, skylight-cut ceiling rose high over a single, large, wood-paneled living room and a very rustic kitchen. A large fireplace sat along one side wall, a few select framed pieces of art hung on the walls, and four bookshelves teemed neatly with both reading material and a choice few knickknacks. One long desk held Sage's computers and paraphernalia, but it was unobtrusive, and the only nod to high-tech modernity. There was no television—all the couches and chairs instead faced the massive triangular floor-to-ceiling window that took up the entire back wall of the house, and looked out through the forest and over a beautifully secluded and pristine strip of beach. Ben and I walked to the window, openmouthed.

"This view . . ." I gaped. "I can't believe you ever leave."

"It takes a lot," Sage admitted.

I tore my eyes from the rolling ocean waves and looked again around the room. It was cozy and intimate, and yet somehow not personal. It reminded me of vacation homes my family used to rent when I was little: tiny touches proved that the house belonged to someone else, but they were few and far between. I was so curious—where was Sage in this house? I was dying to snoop around and check it out.

"Do we get a tour?" I asked.

"No tour. We're here only to get supplies." He pulled a volume from the highest shelf of one of the bookcases. From the spine it looked like a fairly nondescript hardback, but when Sage set it down, I saw it was actually a small combination safe. He undid the lock and pulled open the cover to reveal a large stack of envelopes, each one labeled with a different name: Franklin Hobart, Brian Yancey, Everett Singer, Larry Steczynski . . . it was this last one he grabbed and pulled open, emptying its contents into his wallet and pockets.

"Larry Steczynski?" I asked incredulously.

Sage smiled. "You don't think it suits me?"

"Oh, I think it suits you perfectly. How many aliases do you have?"

"I'm a bit of a collector."

I placed a hand on his wrist, stopping him as he transferred something into his wallet. "Does Larry Steczynski carry a black AmEx?"

"He might."

"My mom doesn't even carry a black AmEx."

"Apparently your mom doesn't move in the same circles as Larry Steczynski."

"Sage," Ben called from across the room. He had knelt down to gaze closely at a sculpted figurine that sat on an end table, and his voice broke with awe. "This . . . this is a real Michelangelo, isn't it?"

"Yeah, yeah it is."

"But it's a *Michelangelo*!"

"Yep."

"And that painting," Ben said, nodding to a piece on the wall featuring a sketch of what looked like a somewhat cherubic version of Sage himself. "That's a real Rubens?"

"It is."

"It looks like you."

"Strong genetics in the family line," Sage explained.

This seemed like a good time to slip out. "Bathroom?" I asked.

Sage pointed across the room to a tiny hall that branched off. The bathroom was there . . . and so was a closed door, just a little farther down the hall. Sage's bedroom—it had to be.

I tiptoed down the hall and eased open the

door, taking great pains to pull it gently closed behind me.

If Sage did sleep here, it was a tight squeeze. The room was packed full of art and supplies: canvases, easels, paints, charcoals . . . some were works in progress, others were on display, and every inch of wall space held a framed image. Scanning them, my heart started to race. Almost every image featured one of four women.

Women I knew.

Women I had been in dreams.

They didn't look like me the way they did when I dreamed about them, but I was absolutely certain who they were.

One woman laughed as she held on to the sides of a rowboat floating on the Tiber—Olivia.

One woman's long red hair flowed wildly behind her as she raced on her horse—Catherine.

One woman studied her face in the mirror, expertly applying stage makeup—Anneline.

One woman leaned against a piano, singing in the middle of a packed audience—Delia.

There was more. A canvas mounted on the wall—a watercolor of two young men in Renaissance clothing, holding absurd stances. I knew this painting. I'd painted it. The men were Sage and Giovanni, and I remembered the dream where I'd tried to get them to keep still and pose.

I looked at the bottom right-hand corner of the piece: signed with a single *O*. Her signature. My signature?

Was it possible? Were my dreams actually . . . memories? Memories of past lives? I didn't believe in reincarnation . . . but what else made sense?

And what about Sage? He looked the same in Olivia's picture as he did now. It seemed strange that he would be reincarnated looking exactly the same and I wouldn't be.

I was grateful when laughter from the other room stopped my wild thoughts. Sage and Ben laughing together? Apparently a lot of strange things happened in this house. I had to get back before they realized how long I'd been gone, but I didn't want to leave. What did all this mean? Could there still be some kind of rational explanation?

Should I ask Sage? He might not like that I'd snooped, but he couldn't get that angry. He was still basically a stranger—I had every right to try and find out more about him.

I had my hand on the doorknob and was about to leave when a canvas in the corner caught my eye.

It wasn't framed, and it wasn't on display. It was on its side, the top canvas in a stack of them, all leaned against the wall. A sheet covered the pile most of the way, but the image of an eye grabbed my attention.

The eye was huge on the page, rendered in a stunning, clear blue. It was beautiful . . . but hauntingly blank. I couldn't tear myself away from the image. I didn't even realize I was walking toward it until I was there, pulling off the sheet.

It was all I could do to stifle a bloodcurdling scream.

Of course the eye was blank. It belonged to Olivia, and she was dead. She was lying on her side, the back of her skull crushed in, and her mouth fixed open in a final scream of terror. Blood pooled all around her; the iris charm she wore was fixed to the floor in a cake of red. The whole canvas drowned in a sea of blood, and while Olivia's body was the focus, it was only the centerpiece of an abattoir of carnage. Other bodies lay behind Olivia's, men and women twisted in poses of horror, swords and daggers impaling them to the floor.

Images from my nightmares flashed through my mind, and I winced away from them. I'd lived this scene.

Oh my God, was I looking at a painting of my own death?

Trembling, I reached out to flip to the next painting. Even touching the canvas made my skin crawl.

The next painting was of Anneline . . . or what had once been Anneline. She was sprawled out in a white bedroom: white curtains billowing in from the open window, white bed linens, white furniture. She was dressed in a flowing white gown. The only color came from her red lips, the long black spread of her hair, the silver of her iris-charm necklace, her unseeing brown eyes . . . and blood. It poured out of her from countless gashes in her torso, and splashed tiny polka dots over the rest of the snowy white landscape.

There was one more horrible piece of red in the picture.

A single long-stemmed rose, pushed deep into her chest, over her heart.

I felt my gorge rise.

I couldn't look anymore.

I had to.

I heard voices from the other room—how long had I been in here? Was Sage coming in? What would he do if he saw me with these?

Quickly I flipped through the other canvases: more of the same. Delia's death pose was pristinely clean, with only a single gaping bullet hole between her eyes. Catherine's was terrible; she writhed and screamed as a bonfire of flames engulfed her waif-like body, tied securely to a stake.

The voices were coming closer. I had to get out of here.

Then I noticed something on the wall. A line of nails. Four of them, each with a delicate iris-charm necklace hanging off it.

And a fifth nail.

Empty.

Waiting.

I raced out of the room and locked myself into the bathroom just in time to lean over the toilet and be sick.

Almost instantly there was a pounding on the door.

"Clea? Are you okay?" Sage's voice rang out. "You've been in there forever."

"I'm sorry," I croaked. "It's my stomach. I don't know why, but—" I felt my gorge rising again, and for the first time ever I was happy someone was going to hear me throw up—it gave me an excuse to stay in here and get it together.

"Ooh, okay. Take your time," Sage said.

I listened to his footsteps as he walked away. When I could I got up to run cold water over my face and rinse out my mouth, but I was still breathing heavily and shaking all over.

Oh my God, was Sage going to kill me?

The paintings didn't necessarily mean that. The ones on the wall were of good times. And hadn't my therapist told me art was great for people who'd lost someone? Maybe that helped him deal. And the necklaces . . . if Sage loved those women, of course he'd keep their most treasured possessions.

Unless he kept them the way serial killers keep souvenirs.

Was Sage a serial killer? Some kind of timeless, ageless serial killer who didn't choose multiple victims, but instead just one . . . and killed her—killed *me*—over and over again?

nine

"CLEA?"

It was Ben's voice this time.

"Are you okay?"

Was I okay? I honestly had no idea. Was I going crazy? Maybe if I could tell Ben what I had seen, he could help me put everything together in a way that made sense. This was all far more his thing than mine.

My dad. I had to concentrate on my dad. Whatever Sage was, he was my only hope for finding my dad. I needed Sage for that, and if I told Ben what I'd discovered, he'd jump to the worst possible conclusion and do everything in his power to keep Sage and I apart.

I had to keep what I'd seen to myself. I had to act like nothing had changed.

"Clea?"

"I'm fine, Ben!"

I finished up, practiced a smile in the mirror, then emerged.

"Sorry about that," I said.

"Are you okay?"

"Yep, I'm fine."

"Did you see that Sage has an original Michelangelo? And a Rubens? And he has an original printing of *Paradise Lost*."

Of course he does, I thought. *He probably knew all of them personally.*

"Wow," I said instead. "He must spend a fortune on eBay."

"Right, because who doesn't buy million-dollar antiquities online?"

"Okay, so maybe not eBay . . ."

"Clea?" Sage's voice rang out as Ben and I walked into the main room, and when I looked up I screamed.

Sage was brandishing a knife.

"Clea? Are you okay?" he asked.

"Yes . . . sorry, I just . . . that's a huge knife."

He laughed. "I heated up a turkey I had in the fridge. I was going to make us sandwiches. Does that work for you?"

A turkey. The knife was for a turkey.

"Yeah, that's great. Thanks." I pasted on a smile.

Sage went back to carving the bird, but looked at me like I'd lost my mind. "Maybe we should take you to a doctor."

"I'm fine. Just a little disoriented from . . . you know."

"Right."

Somehow I managed to keep hold of my sanity for the next fifteen minutes. Sage finished making sandwiches, double-checked to make sure he had all Larry Steczynski's necessary documents, and put together a small duffel bag of clothes. Every time he looked my way, I couldn't help but feel that he knew exactly what I'd seen and done. He didn't like it, and he'd find a way to make me pay.

Once we got out of the house, I felt like I could breathe again. I stuck close to Ben as the three of us made the short, moonlit trek to the garage. No way was I sitting next to Sage. I told Ben to ride shotgun and pretended I still felt a little nauseous so I wouldn't have to talk.

Had Sage and I been reincarnated again and again over the centuries, only to wind up together each time? In a way it would make sense, except I'd been four different women that I knew of and he'd been . . . Sage. So that meant he'd what? Been alive for the last five hundred years?

I inwardly rolled my eyes at my own absurdity, then realized that all my other options were just as absurd. There was the incubus theory, but could spirits bleed? I wasn't as up on these things as Ben, but I thought by definition a "spirit" wasn't something that could bleed. I'd seen Sage bleed. I'd *made* Sage bleed. Not that it hurt him any; he healed so quickly. . . .

In smaller doses it has incredible healing powers. Ben's voice rang out in my head. I remembered he said that earlier, about . . . the Elixir of Life.

The crackpot, completely bogus, absolutely insane Elixir of Life.

Did it actually exist? Had Sage had some? Enough to keep him alive, young, and speed-healing for the last five hundred years?

And if so, had he used that time to find one woman, again and again in different incarnations, to love her . . . or destroy her?

We pulled into a drugstore near the airport so

Larry Steczynski could buy me a pair of cheap shoes, and get both Ben and me duffel bags full of whatever we wanted to pass off as luggage. Buying one-way tickets from Rio to New York and traveling without any luggage would definitely raise red flags.

As we shopped, I pushed my suspicions aside so I could act something akin to normal. I was quickly losing sight of what "normal" might be. When we arrived at the airport, Mr. Steczynski munificently used his black AmEx to treat all three of us to first-class seats on the next flight to JFK.

I had barely said two words to Sage since my discovery. I worried that he'd notice I was acting differently. I racked my brain for something natural to say to him, but by the time we got to our gate, all I'd come up with was, "So . . . how exactly will we get to the house if people are watching and waiting for us?"

"I'm not sure yet."

"Oh, good." Ben nodded. "Excellent that we're following you, then."

"How about I call Rayna?" I said. "She can pick us up. We'll duck down in the car so no one can see us when we drive onto the property, she'll pull right into the garage, and we'll be in."

"And if someone's waiting for us inside?" Ben asked.

"They don't know for sure we're coming—why would they risk breaking in?"

"I guess . . . ," Ben mused.

"You have a better option?"

He didn't. Neither did Sage. I borrowed Larry Steczynski's cell phone to call Rayna. Personally, I never answer the phone if I don't recognize the number. Rayna doesn't feel the same way; she sees an unknown caller as a doorway to a possible romance.

"Hello?" she answered seductively.

"Hey, it's me."

"Clea! Are you okay? I've been phone-stalking you for days. What happened? Where have you been?"

"Sorry, I lost my cell. Everything's okay." Wow—that was easily the biggest lie I'd ever told anyone in my life

"*How* okay?" she asked playfully. "Did you meet someone amazing at Carnival and get swept off your feet?"

I loved that those were the only two options for Rayna: Either something had gone horribly wrong, or I'd gotten wrapped up in a wild, whirlwind romance.

I glanced at Sage. "I *did* meet someone. . . ."

"I knew it! I want to know everything."

"It's kind of a long story."

"I've got nothing but time. Details!"

"It's complicated. Here's the thing, though: Ben and I are in some trouble, and it has to do with my dad."

"What happened?"

"I'll tell you everything, but I need a huge favor. I need you to pick us up at JFK in the morning, and I need you to please not say anything about us coming. I know it sounds crazy, but I think there might be people watching the house and waiting for us to show up."

"Really? I haven't seen anything."

"Good. Hopefully I'm wrong. Can you do it?"

"Of course. Be careful."

"I promise." I gave her our flight information, and we hung up. I glanced over at Ben and Sage. Whatever camaraderie they'd found over Sage's art and literature collection hadn't lasted. It seemed the reality of Sage coming to Ben's turf was too much for Ben to take, and they now sat next to each other, facing forward, without acknowledging each other, absolute stones. I imagined the twelve-hour trip ahead of us, me playing buffer between the two of them even as I struggled to deal with my own suspicions about Sage. I was exhausted just thinking about it. I decided to wander the terminal stores, and grinned as I found the perfect thing.

I waited until we were on the plane before I showed off my purchase.

"Cribbage!" I declared, pulling out the board, a deck of cards, and pen and paper, "Ben and I are going to teach you. Then we can all play."

"What makes you think I don't know how to play cribbage?" Sage asked.

"You do?" Ben sounded surprised.

"I happen to be an *excellent* cribbage player," Sage said.

"Really . . . because I'm what one might call a cribbage master," Ben said.

"I bet I've been playing longer than you," Sage said, and I cast my eyes his way. Was he trying to tell us something?

"I highly doubt that," Ben said, "but I believe we'll see the proof when I double-skunk you."

"Clearly you're both forgetting it's a three-person game, and I'm ready to destroy you both," I said.

"Deal 'em," Ben said.

Being a horse person, my mother was absolutely convinced she could achieve world peace if she just got the right parties together on a long enough ride. I didn't know about that, but apparently cribbage might do the trick. The three of us were pretty evenly matched, and Ben was impressed enough to ask Sage how he learned to play. Turned out Sage's parents were historians, he said, so they first taught him the precursor to cribbage, a game called noddy.

"Really?" Ben asked, his professional curiosity piqued. "Your parents were historians? Did they teach?"

"European history. In Europe," Sage said. "Small college. They taught me a lot."

Yep, there was the metaphorical gauntlet. I saw the gleam in Ben's eye as he picked it up. "Interesting," he said. "So you'd say you know a lot about European history?"

"I would say that. In fact, I believe I just did say that."

Ben grinned, and immediately set out to expose Sage as an intellectual fraud. He'd ask questions to trip Sage up and test his story, things I had no idea were tests until I heard Sage's reactions.

"So which of Shakespeare's plays do you think

was better served by the Globe Theatre: *Henry VIII* or *Troilus and Cressida*?" Ben asked, cracking his knuckles.

"*Troilus and Cressida* was never performed at the Globe," Sage replied. "As for *Henry VIII,* the original Globe caught fire during the show and burned to the ground, so I'd say that's the show that really brought down the house . . . wouldn't you?"

"Nice . . . very nice." Ben nodded. "Well done."

It was the cerebral version of bamboo under the fingernails, and while they both tried to seem casual about their conversation, they were soon leaning forward with sweat beading on their brows. It was fascinating . . . and weird.

After several hours of this, Ben had to admit that he'd found a historical peer, and he gleefully involved Sage in all kinds of debates about the minutiae of eras I knew nothing about . . . except that I had the nagging sense I might have been there for some of them.

For his part, Sage seemed to relish talking about the past with someone who could truly appreciate the detailed anecdotes and stories he'd discovered in his "research." By the time we started our descent into Miami, the two were leaning over my seat to chat and laugh together. On the very full flight from Miami to New York, Ben and Sage took the two seats next to each other and gabbed and giggled like middle-school girls. I sat across from them stuck next to an older woman wearing far too much perfume.

I wondered if Ben would have enjoyed the conversation more or less if I'd told him I suspected Sage was speaking from memory, not from education.

I was glad they were talking—it gave me a chance to get my thoughts together. I felt so drawn to Sage. I felt like he was meant to be in my life. I *wanted* to be around him. Why would I feel that way if he'd killed me in the past? Didn't it make more sense that he hadn't? That would explain why he always looked so haunted: Every woman he loved was killed.

Was I going to die too?

I faded in and out of a light sleep as I thought through it all. There was so much I didn't understand. Like the photographs. I believed Sage when he'd sounded surprised that he'd been in my pictures. He said he'd never seen me before we met on the beach. So why had he been in my pictures from the day I was born? Could that be a sign of some kind of spiritual connection that brought us together lifetime after lifetime? Rayna would love that story. I wondered what Ben would think of it. Even more, what would my dad think?

Actually, I kind of knew what my dad thought. He wanted to help Sage. He even told Sage he was a good man. So I should trust that, right?

Unless my dad wanted the Elixir so badly he didn't care if Sage was good or bad, and just said what he needed to say.

The whole thing made my head hurt.

I turned to the heavily perfumed woman.

"You like cribbage?" I offered.

Two hours and an excruciatingly long game of War later (she didn't play cribbage, but she just *loved* War), we landed at JFK. Rayna was waiting for us in baggage claim.

"CLEA!!" she screamed, and threw herself into my arms. It wasn't exactly inconspicuous, but I didn't care. I hugged her fiercely in return. She pulled away and saw Sage, and her eyes went completely round.

"Is this the trouble you're in?" she asked, looking him up and down. "I so approve."

"Rayna, this is Sage. Sage, Rayna."

"Pleased to meet you," Sage said, offering his hand.

"The pleasure is all mine," Rayna purred. "Unless, of course, it's all Clea's, which is even better."

Sage smiled and might have even blushed a bit, which was highly entertaining.

Before leading us to the car, Rayna insisted I take her heavy winter coat. It was thirty-four degrees outside, and I was still wearing my little black sundress. Of course, Rayna herself was wearing a lacy push-up camisole. She took Sage's arm "to keep her steady on the ice," though I think her main goal was to see if his arm was as muscular as it looked. By the openmouthed gape she shot me after her first squeeze, it was.

"They'd make a cute couple," Ben said, nodding to Sage and Rayna. "Don't you think?"

I settled for a noncommittal "Hmm."

In the car, I slipped into the front seat beside Rayna. With only her eyes, she asked me if Sage was mine. With a scrunch of my nose and a shrug, I explained it was complicated. She nodded—she understood—then gave an eye roll that clearly said I was insane if I did anything but jump at the chance to be with him. The whole conversation took about a second.

On the two-and-a-half-hour drive to Niantic, I filled Rayna in on as much as I could—pretty much everything except my dreams and what I'd found at Sage's house. It was a lot of highly bizarre stuff, but Rayna took it all in stride. At least now she understood why we had to be so careful about getting into the house.

"This is perfect!" Rayna said. "You could not have picked a better day to come home."

"What do you mean?" I asked.

"Your mom called this morning. Some big government figure is visiting from Israel, and your mom decided they'll get the most accomplished over a giant impromptu Piri-catered lunch at the house."

Amazing. Only my mom could manage a last-minute luncheon for a group of dignitaries whose schedules had probably been etched in stone for months. It was the kind of unheard-of thing she had become famous for during her time in Washington.

"So you mean . . . ," I started.

But Rayna finished for me, laughing as she said, "The Secret Service showed up at six this morning to go over the whole property with microscopes, and they're not leaving until the party's over. If there were dangerous people anywhere near the house, they're either long gone or in federal custody."

Excellent—I couldn't have planned it better. I spun around in my seat.

"Gird yourself, Sage," I chirped. "I guarantee nothing you've ever experienced has prepared you for Piri and my mom in action."

"I'm sure they're impressive," Sage said.

Clearly, he had no idea. He'd learn.

Rayna was right. The Secret Service was all over the house. They knew Ben and Rayna, but "Larry Steczynski" had to be properly vetted. If there was any doubt about the authenticity of his fake ID, it would now be put to the test. As Sage waited for the Secret Service to do their due diligence, I wondered how much our mission to find Dad would be set back by Sage taking a quick detour to federal prison.

"He's clear," the lead agent finally said.

Great, we could go in. Sage politely insisted that Rayna and I enter before him.

"Not sure that's such a good idea," I said, but he wouldn't hear it. Rayna, Ben, and I shared a knowing smile. Then I shrugged and stepped over the threshold . . . immediately triggering the Piri alarm. I don't know how she knew; she was all the way in the kitchen. But the minute I stepped into the foyer she raced in, arms waving in the air, a high-pitched scream keening from her lungs.

"AIIIIIIEEEEEEEEE!!"

"He made me do it, Piri," I said, happily tossing Sage under the bus. "I tried to tell him—"

Piri strode right up to Sage, her head barely reaching his sternum, and jabbed her finger into his chest to emphasize each scolding word. "You never let a woman enter this house before a man! Very bad luck! And when the senator's doing business! Jaj!"

She pushed us back outside, closed the door, and spit three times on the porch (barely missing the shoes of one of the Secret Service agents), then turned her baleful eyes to Sage, asking him to do the same.

"I don't think I really need to spit on Clea's porch," Sage said uncomfortably, but Piri's glare only grew more and more violent until he withered under its power . . . and spit three times. Piri smiled smugly and opened the door, gesturing for Sage to enter. Ben went next, bending to Piri's ear to murmur, "If it'd been me, I would have gone in first."

"That's because you're a smart boy," Piri said, kissing him on both cheeks.

Once we were all in, Piri greeted us as if for the first time, with huge hugs and two-cheeked kisses.

As she led us to the luncheon raging in the other room, Ben crowed to Sage, "You know, a *real* European scholar would be up on old-school superstitions."

Sage grimaced.

Mom's party wasn't huge, but the simple force of all the personalities made it feel like the room was filled with people. As was often the case, Mom was the only woman at the party. Her guests included seven top members of the Senate Foreign Relations Committee, and a man I'm sure I should have recognized but didn't, whom I imagined was the Israeli diplomat. They were all feasting from trays that groaned under the weight of traditional Hungarian appetizers like *langos* (bread puffs with garlic, sour cream, and cheese), several kinds of *pogacsa* (biscuits), *körözött* (cheese spread with Hungarian paprika), and *fasirt* (meatballs). Everyone sat except my mom, who was in the middle of acting out a very colorful story about a horse ride she'd taken with another foreign diplomat.

"So I turn around, and his shirt is off!" she exclaimed. "I mean, even the horse is flabbergasted, but the press is eating it up, snapping picture after picture. Then he pounds on his chest and cries out, 'Vigorous Torso, the people call me! Vigorous Torso!' Then he challenges me to a *wrestling* match!"

Everyone laughed, and she rolled her eyes dramatically. Then Senator Blaine from Delaware, my mom's best friend on the committee, gave her the setup she awaited.

"Did you do it?"

"Oh hell yes. Took him down in ten seconds."

Everyone laughed harder, and Mom raised her shot glass in a toast to them all and downed her *pálinka,* the Hungarian brandy Piri had brought out for the occasion. Mom took a bow as everyone applauded, and collapsed dramatically into her seat.

Then she saw me.

"Clea!" she cried. "Come here!"

I grinned and ran to her, and she wrapped me in a fierce hug. "I've missed you, baby!" She pulled away and spun me around to face the group, her hands on my shoulders. "Everyone, I'm sure you remember my incredibly accomplished daughter,

Clea, who we'll all be working for one day. Clea, you know the senators, and this is Imi Sanders, Israeli minister of foreign affairs."

"Pleased to meet you," I said, shaking the minister's hand.

"The pleasure is mine, " he replied.

"Of course you've also all met Rayna"—Mom pointed Rayna out to the crowd—"and Clea's friend Ben, and . . ." She eyed Sage suspiciously. "Who might this young man be?"

In an instant I sorted through every possible explanation for Sage's presence, but judging by the way Mom was looking at him, I knew she already had it in her head that he was a romantic prospect, and she'd go on believing that even if I said he was purely a homeschool friend. And if she thought I was interested in him, no political luncheon would stop her from sitting us down and grilling Sage in front of everyone so she could dig up any deal breakers before I had to find them out the hard way. She'd probably even encourage her guests to join in, and I knew they'd be happy to do it—I'd seen it happen to Rayna.

The problem was, I couldn't spend all day hanging out at Mom's lunch. I needed to go through

Dad's things, and I wanted to finish before the Israeli minister and his Secret Service protection left the house open for any not-so-welcome visitors to return.

"This is Larry Steczynski! You can call him Sage. He's my new boyfriend!" Rayna suddenly chirped, threading her arm through Sage's and giving him a squeeze. To his credit, Sage looked only slightly surprised.

Just one more thing to add to the long list of reasons I love Rayna. She knew exactly what I'd been thinking and had found the one answer that would leave me completely off the hook.

"Really!" Mom said meaningfully. "Then we should talk." She turned to the group and asked, "Gentlemen?"

Without hesitation, all the senators and the Israeli minister agreed that the next topic of their agenda should clearly be a debate of Sage's merits and pitfalls as a partner to Rayna. As Mom took Sage and Rayna's hands and led them to the couch, two senators gladly moved aside to give them space. Sage shot me a look so plaintive I almost laughed out loud.

"Ben and I will be back in a bit," I said. "We have some Alissa Grande stuff to go over."

"Don't take too long," Mom called as we left the room. "We're flying back to Washington in a couple hours and I want to see you before I go. I've almost forgotten what you look like."

I promised her we'd be quick, and Ben and I slipped away, just in time to hear Senator Blaine clear his throat and say, "So, Sage . . . what if any personal views about women do you have that might interfere with your obligation to treat Rayna with the respect that she deserves?"

"He may have faced down swarms of crazed New Age militants," I whispered to Ben, "but I bet this is his first Senate confirmation hearing."

"It's cruel and unusual punishment, Clea," Ben said, smiling, "but I like it."

"I'm thinking anything that has to do with the Elixir of Life would be in Dad's studio, right?" I asked.

Ben nodded. "Let's start there."

We went down to the studio, opened the door, and just stared at the mountains of papers, books, and binders.

"This could take a lifetime," I said.

"We just have to be smart about it. We'll look through all his stuff that's specifically about the Elixir first. I'll call up the computer files so you can go through those. I'll go through the handwritten stuff."

"So we should be looking through it all for some kind of reference to a darker-skinned woman?" I asked.

"A darker-skinned woman?"

"Well, Sage said 'a dark lady.' I really can't imagine Dad would have said that. I can't imagine anyone would have said that, but I guess if Sage lived—"

"Guess if Sage lived what?" Ben asked.

I'd been about to say that Sage was most likely born in the 1500s, so he might slip sometimes when it came to what was and was not appropriate, but I hadn't brought Ben in on that theory yet, and we definitely didn't have the time right now.

"Sage might have paraphrased," I covered. "He must have."

"Right. That makes sense. So a woman who's not Caucasian."

All the Elixir of Life computer files were pulled up, and I sifted through them as Ben flipped through notebooks.

After two hours, we'd found all kinds of information about the Elixir, its history, and its powers.

I even found a file all about the two groups Sage had told us were after him: Cursed Vengeance and the Saviors of Eternal Life.

Cursed Vengeance got its name because its members believed their bloodlines had somehow been cursed by the Elixir for generations. They believed that if they found and destroyed it, they could save themselves. The Saviors of Eternal Life wanted the Elixir for the opposite reason: They believed it was their duty to keep it safe and decide how best to use its powers.

Dad's file backed up what Sage had said—that both groups had origins in the Renaissance, but got much stronger when Dad found the vials. While both groups sprawled out across the world, they stayed unified through several encrypted websites. Dad had a list of some of them, and he'd even found the pass code for one. I checked it out. It belonged to the Saviors of Eternal Life. It was a chat forum, basically, where members could share information with one another. The posts were pretty sporadic—I got the idea that this particular site wasn't a main hub for the group. Still, I printed out the site address and code. It couldn't hurt to have as much information on our enemies as possible.

Unfortunately, neither Ben nor I had seen anything about a darker-skinned woman, and time was running out. Mom's party, and the protection it provided, could end at any time.

"This is crazy. We're getting nowhere," I said.

"I know." Ben looked frazzled and disheveled, and he ran his hands through his hair. "We need another idea."

We thought . . . but we both came up empty.

"Okay," I finally considered out loud, "maybe 'dark lady' isn't actually a person. Maybe it's a code word."

"A code word?"

"Maybe. Maybe the letters stand for other letters. Or maybe it's like an acrostic, where each letter is part of another word. I don't know. . . . I'm reaching . . . I'm getting punchy . . . maybe I should start drinking coffee."

"No, no, it's good. A code is good. It could be something hidden in literature, even. Literature is full of codes. Like Shakespeare's sonnets." Ben suddenly bolted up, like he'd been struck with a cattle prod. "Oh my God!"

"What?"

"Shakespeare's sonnets! The Dark Lady! He wrote twenty-seven sonnets about a woman called the Dark Lady! I can't believe I didn't think of that!"

"Yes!" I jumped in. "And Dad was obsessed with Shakespeare before he disappeared!"

Ben and I looked at each other a moment, then we both dug into Dad's piles, searching for all his books on Shakespeare. He'd filled them with notations and highlights, most of them surrounding the Dark Lady, but there wasn't anything we could use, just a lot of asterisks, arrows, and underlinings.

"I keep seeing the words 'see file,'" I told Ben.

"Me too." He lifted his head to look at me. "Computer file?"

I raced back to the computer, and we scanned his folders until we saw one labeled "Shakespeare." In that was a folder labeled "Dark Lady," and in *that* was a Word document named "DLLXR.doc."

"*D*ark *L*ady *L-X-R* . . . Dark Lady Elixir!" I cried.

"YES!" Ben cheered, and we took a second for a nerdy high five before we opened the file.

"'This file is password protected,'" I read.

"Come on!" Ben groaned.

"Passwords . . . what are Dad's passwords? He wrote down all his passwords, he couldn't remember anything. Look around, and I'll try some things."

Ben knew the way Dad kept his passwords: printed on labels and stuck on the inside of drawers and cabinets. Ben opened everything and wrote them down, while I tried every kind of password I could imagine might have meaning to my father. I tried several combinations of my name, Mom's name, Dad's name, Rayna and Ben's names, our birthdays, the word GloboReach, the date GloboReach was formed, Mom and Dad's anniversary. . . .

"Nothing. I'm getting nothing," I snapped, frustrated. "Now what?"

"Wait, wait, I've got some," Ben said. He read out a list of over twenty passwords. None of them were right.

"This sucks! The one file on the whole computer that's password protected!"

"Exactly," Ben said. "Let's think about this. Why would Grant password-protect this one file?"

"To frustrate his daughter and her best friend to no end?"

"Good guess, but probably not."

"Because it's important."

"Right," he said. "Your dad believes in the Elixir. It's everything for him—he finds it and he changes the world. The wrong people find it and bad shit goes down. So if this file is the key to finding it, of course he password-protects it."

"But we already looked through all his passwords."

"We looked in his usual places," Ben said. "Something this important, he'd want somewhere really safe—somewhere only he could get to it, and it would be with him all the time."

"Like where?" I asked. "The only thing that's with him all the time is . . ."

Ben and I both realized it at the same time, but I said it out loud.

"His watch!"

Immediately I dug into my camera case and pulled out his watch. I studied it all over, searching for anything that could be a password. Mom's inscription, maybe? I looked at it, then noticed the tiny scratches underneath the words.

"What do you think about this?" I asked, showing it to Ben. "Are they just scratches?"

"I'm not sure . . . it's so small . . ."

"A loupe!" I remembered. "Dad has a loupe here to magnify pictures!"

Ben ransacked drawers until he shouted, "I got it!"

He tossed me the loupe, and I looked closely at the scratches. They read "faithvalorwisdom." Faith, valor, and wisdom—the three petals of the iris. I grinned and entered it in the box on the computer.

"We're in!" I cried.

Ben joined me and read over my shoulder as we scanned the file. There was a ton of material, but the gist of it was that while Dad was researching the Elixir of Life, he'd found an obscure reference book that tied the Elixir to Shakespeare. The book cited a lost play in Shakespeare's canon: *Love's Labour's Wonne*. Only the title remained, and while many assumed from that title that the play was a sequel to *Love's Labour's Lost,* Dad's reference book said it was actually a story about a pair of lovers brought together and then ripped apart because of the Elixir of Life. Furthermore, the book said the story was inspired by a lover of Shakespeare's—the Dark Lady.

From there, Dad did more research. He wanted to know who the Dark Lady was, to see if she might have some connection to the Elixir. Dad pored over volumes of analysis on the subject, as well as the sonnets themselves. After exhaustive study, he wound up rejecting all the mainstream theories about the Dark Lady's identity. He believed the Dark Lady was a woman named Magda Alessandri, whom many thought to be a sorceress. Dad wondered if her reputation as a sorceress came from an entanglement with the Elixir of Life, and he tried to find out more about her. He even managed to track down her living descendants, and had been visiting and interviewing them during his trips to various GloboReach outposts around the world.

At the very bottom of the document, Dad had written "EUREKA CURRENT MAGDA ALESSANDRI CLEA'S ROOM 121."

"You think he found the descendant of the Dark Lady he was looking for?" I asked Ben.

He nodded. "And her name is also Magda Alessandri. But what's 'Clea's Room One-Twenty-One'?"

"Another code? Double protection for the woman's location? Did he hide it somewhere in my room?"

We looked at each other and raced out of the studio and up the two flights of stairs to my room. Once we got there, I flipped on my computer. "Maybe he put a file on here."

Ben nodded. "Look for any file you didn't make. Maybe it's password protected with 'one-twenty-one.'"

I agreed, but after a half hour of scouring my computer, I found nothing on the hard drive that I hadn't put there.

"No!" I cried. "Come on . . . we're so close!"

"Don't get frustrated. It has to be something else. One-twenty-one . . . a date, maybe? January twenty-first? Or is it twelve-one—December first? Check iCal—maybe he put something there."

"Nothing," I shook my head. "Now what?"

"I don't know. Maybe we're wrong about the computer." Ben's eyes darted desperately around the room for inspiration.

"Clea!" Mom's voice rang out from downstairs. "Come on down! We're breaking up, and I want to see you before we go!"

Ugh, we were doomed. The Secret Service was about to leave, and we still had no idea—

"Cribbage!" Ben raced to the cribbage board and grabbed it. "What's the final score in cribbage?"

"One-twenty-one," I said, then my eyes widened as I realized, "One-twenty-one—that's it!"

Ben looked all over the board, then turned it

upside down and slid away the metal panel that closed the peg compartment. He dumped the pegs into his hand, looked inside, and closed his eyes . . . in defeat?

"Ben?" I asked nervously.

He grinned and held up the board so I could see it. Written very small inside the peg compartment were two numbers stacked on top of each other. The bottom one began with a minus sign, and both included decimal points. Below them was written, "Little Door."

"What are the numbers? An equation?" I asked.

Ben's grin spread even wider. "Coordinates. Latitude and longitude."

"The location of the 'current Magda Alessandri'!"

Ben nodded. I screamed and threw myself into his arms.

"Clea?" Mom called.

"Coming!"

Knowing there was a good chance we'd be away from the house for a while, I grabbed a duffel bag and tossed some clothes inside. I also threw in some makeup. There was no reason I had to look like a fugitive just because I'd be acting like one. I rummaged through my purses and grabbed any cash I had. I was sure Larry Steczynski's black

AmEx would cover us, but I liked having my own money, even if it was just a little bit. The last thing I threw in was my cribbage board with the secret coordinates inside.

Mission accomplished, we raced downstairs and into the foyer just as everyone was leaving. Rayna beamed as she hugged everyone good-bye and accepted their wishes for a long and happy relationship. Sage looked dazed.

"How did it go?" I asked.

"I think your mother just arranged peace in the Middle East while brokering a marriage deal for Rayna and me."

"I'm not surprised. How many kids are you having?"

"Four. But we can't start until she's twenty-six, three years after the wedding. Oh, and we're honey-mooning at the minister's beach house in Tel Aviv."

"That's nice. I'll have to pop in for a visit."

Sage just shook his head, still shell-shocked.

"Piri forgive you yet?" Ben grinned.

"I don't think so. She put an inch of garlic on everything she served me."

"Don't take it personally. There's lots of garlic in Hungarian food," I assured him.

"Including my chocolate torte," Sage added.

"Okay, you can take that personally," I admitted.

Mom was the last of the politicos left in the house, and she turned to me with a sad pout on her face. "I can't believe I barely got to see you and now I'm leaving!"

"I know! Here—we'll walk out with you. We're leaving too." I didn't want to be anywhere near the house for even a second after the Secret Service left.

"You didn't even get any of Piri's desserts," Mom lamented as the five of us walked out the door. "She made Hungarian butterhorns with apricots. Your favorite."

"Were there any left?"

"I think a few. You may have lucked out," Mom said.

"I'll get 'em." Ben tried to walk back inside, but Piri blocked his way.

"NO!" she screamed. "Never turn back when you leave the house. Very, very bad luck."

"It's fine, Piri," Ben assured her. "I just want to grab the cookies."

"I'll get them. You come here and look in the mirror. Give a dirty look, then everything's better."

"I would, I swear, you know I would, Piri, but

we're kind of in a rush. I'll just grab the cookies."

As Ben pushed past her and went inside, Mom hugged both Rayna and Sage, who apparently was going to be like a son-in-law to her. Ben loped out with the butterhorns, and everyone climbed into Rayna's car, then Mom and I gave each other one last hug.

"I have a big recess in April," she said, holding my arms and looking into my eyes. "Let's take a whole week and go someplace, just the two of us."

"I'd love that," I said, willing myself not to well up. Mom couldn't take that. We ducked into our respective cars and drove away.

"Butterhorn?" Ben asked, holding out a bag full of the pastries.

"Well, you did condemn yourself to bad luck just to get them for me," I said, "So absolutely!"

"Yeah," Ben agreed, "they'd better be worth it."

"Mmmm, completely worth it," I said with my mouth full. "The rest of you have to have some of these."

"Hmmm," Sage mused, examining his, "no garlic. I'm not entirely sure my taste buds will know how to handle this."

"Um, you guys," Rayna asked, "where am I driving?"

"Excellent question—let's find out!" I pulled the cribbage board out of my duffel bag and handed it to Sage, pointing out the longitude and latitude notations on the back. "Where is that?"

Sage took out his phone, then entered the coordinates. "Interesting."

"What?" I asked. "It's not Antarctica, is it? I didn't pack a parka."

"The coordinates are for a building called 'Shibuya 109' in Tokyo."

"Shibuya 109?" Rayna asked. "The mall?"

Shibuya 109 was indeed a mall, but that couldn't be right . . . could it? Then I had an idea.

"Sage, can I see your phone?" I asked. He gave it to me and I surfed to a listing of all the stores located there.

Amazing.

"You'll never believe this, Ben," I said. "There's a store in Shibuya 109 named 'The Little Door.'"

Ben's eyes went wide. "'The Little Door' . . . like what Grant wrote under the coordinates!"

"Exactly!" I said. "Could that be where Magda works?"

"Magda?" Sage asked.

"Magda Alessandri, the Dark Lady's descendant! That's who my dad wanted you to see!"

"Magda . . . Alessandri?" Sage asked.

"We're really going to Shibuya 109?" Rayna asked. "Is it completely wrong to spend my graduation money four months before I get it?"

"*We* are not going to Shibuya 109," I corrected her. "You have school. Wanda would kill you for skipping. And she'd kill me for helping you."

"It's an educational experience. I'll write a report about it when I get back."

"It could be dangerous, Rayna."

"How dangerous can it be? You're going shopping."

We weren't, but I understood what she meant. Shibuya 109 was the fashion pinnacle for Tokyo's young and hip: ten floors of the most trend-setting shops and boutiques, all packaged in a giant cylindrical building that leaped out of the skyline. Rayna and I had done quite a bit of damage there on our last visit, but that was three years ago, and another onslaught was definitely in our future.

Yet as much as I was dying to attack the place with Rayna by my side, this wasn't the time. While it didn't seem dangerous to look for someone in a department store, nothing on this journey had been what it seemed. This was maybe the only time in my life when I desperately *didn't* want Rayna to be with me.

"Please don't fight me on this, Rayna. If you come with us and something happens—"

She heard how upset I was, and the playful fight left her voice. "It's okay," she said, "you go. I'll stay here . . . pining for my fiancé." She said the last part with practiced melodrama, and I laughed with relief—both that she understood and that she'd be safe at home. As Rayna turned the car onto the highway and headed toward the airport, I turned on the car radio, leaned back in my seat, took a big, meltingly sweet bite of butterhorn, and let the taste linger on my tongue. For this one brief moment, life was simple and filled with joy. I wanted to savor it. I knew it wouldn't last.

ten

IT TURNED OUT I'd have a little more time to enjoy things before we left. The fastest way to get to Tokyo was a direct flight from New York, but it didn't leave until almost two the next afternoon. Sleeping at home wasn't an option, and while Rayna waxed rhapsodic about making the most of Larry Steczynski's black AmEx and treating ourselves like sultans for the night at a cool hotel in Manhattan, it made much more sense to just grab a decent room near the airport.

"Okay," Rayna agreed, "but seriously, we're not going to just go to sleep, right? We need to all hang out. *After* I get some time with Clea. I'm having serious withdrawal."

"You're staying the night with us?" I asked excitedly.

"Hello—did you honestly think I wouldn't? I was serious about the black AmEx fest. But a little hotel will be great too. We'll do Holiday Inn Express. They have amazing cinnamon rolls."

"They do?" I asked.

"*Signature* cinnamon rolls. All you can eat at breakfast."

"I kinda love that you know that."

Aside from cinnamon rolls, Rayna's other request was that she check us in and set up the rooms: two rooms, each with two queen beds, on the same floor, but all the way down the hall from each other. I cringed, imagining Sage and Ben stuck in a room together all night. I couldn't imagine how that would work.

Rayna waited until we got into our room, then threw herself on one of the beds. "Finally! I thought we'd never get a second alone!" Sprawled on her stomach, she propped herself up on her elbows and kicked up her feet. "Spill—what's the deal with Hottie McDreamMan?"

"Sage?" I laughed.

"No, I mean Minister Sanders." She threw a pillow at me. "Of course I mean Sage! He's the one, right? The guy from your dreams. Oh my God—he's real and he's *hot*! Does he kiss as well in real life as he did in your dreams?"

"I wouldn't know," I admitted. "We haven't kissed."

"What are you *waiting* for?"

"So the whole randomly-popping-up-in-pictures thing doesn't bother you?"

"Nope."

"The whole strange-cultists-chasing-after-him? That doesn't bother you either?"

"Nobody's perfect, Clea."

"How about if I told you he might be a serial killer? Would that bother you?"

"Debatable. Elaborate."

I told her about the nightmares and about what I'd seen in his house. As I unrolled the story, her expression went from flip and giddy to open-mouthed and riveted.

"Oh my God, Clea."

"Crazy, right? And I still have no idea how he got into all those pictures."

"That part's easy."

"Really?"

"Of course," she said. "You're soulmates."

"Rayna . . ."

"Fine, I know, you don't like that word. But you can't possibly deny that you have a deep, powerful soul *connection*. By definition you have that. You said yourself, he found you in four different countries and four different times. Out of all the people in the world at any given time, he found *you*. The only possible way he could have done that is if your souls were connected. He's a soul-seeking missile."

"But he told me he wasn't there for any of the pictures."

"Yes, he was! Don't you get it, Clea? Your souls are connected—he's *always* with you, whether he's there physically or not. And you're the one who told me about cameras capturing people's souls, right? So that's what it's doing—capturing the soul that's always with you, because you're always connected. It's *very* romantic."

I thought about what she said, ignoring the last sentence because I knew by now that everything was *very* romantic to Rayna.

"Okay," I ceded, "I'll give you the connection. But what about the serial killer thing? What if we're connected because he tracks these women down, acts like he loves them, and then kills them?"

"Kills you. You're them."

"Yeah, thanks, that's a much nicer way to put it," I said, rolling my eyes.

Rayna considered it a second, then shook her head. "Nope. I don't buy it, Clea."

"Why, because it's not as romantic?"

"It's *not* as romantic, but that's not why I don't buy it. If he's a killer, there are lots of other girls to kill."

"Maybe that's his game, though," I said. "The hunt for one soul, again and again."

"Then why are you still here?"

"The other women lived with him for a long time too. Maybe he wants to wait until my defenses are down, and then—"

"Wow, Clea, you are so jaded. You found your soulmate. People wait their whole lives for this. It's the most amazing thing in the world, and it's happened to you. Can't you just accept it and be happy?"

What she said made sense, but . . .

I flopped back on the bed and stared at the ceiling. Without looking at Rayna, I said, "He doesn't act like he's my soulmate. Sometimes I think maybe he liked the other women more. I think maybe he wishes I was one of them."

Rayna was silent. This was something I'd never heard. "This is seriously deep," she finally said. "You're feeling insecure because you're jealous . . . of yourself."

"I didn't say I was jealous . . ."

"You'd rather think he's a serial killer than risk being with him and finding out he doesn't like you as much as he liked . . . you!" She scrunched her brow and thought, then tried again. "Yous? Anyway, you know what I mean—the other yous."

"Forget the jealousy thing, okay? There are other reasons to doubt him too. Ben doesn't trust him at all. He thinks Sage is some kind of demon. He said there's a spirit called an incubus that comes to women in their sleep, and—"

"Of course Ben said that." Rayna shrugged. "He's jealous."

"Of what?"

"Ben's crazy in love with you, Clea. I've been saying that forever!"

"And I've been ignoring you forever, because it's not true. You just want it to be true because it's romantic."

"Did you not see the pictures of you from Rio?"

I narrowed my eyes. "What are you talking about?"

Rayna pulled out her phone. "Honestly, I don't know how you survive without Google Alerts on yourself. The paparazzi were out in full force for Carnival."

She played with the phone for a minute, then handed it to me. It showed a close-up of Ben and me at the Sambadrome that could only have been taken with a serious zoom. I felt violated.

"I hate this," I muttered.

"Why? You look cute!"

"I hate that people are sneaking around taking pictures of me!"

"I know you do. Ignore that for the moment. Just scroll through."

There were five pictures of Ben and me. Four of them were moments I vividly remembered, pictures of the two of us facing each other, laughing as we did our best to imitate the dancers shimmying and strutting down the parade route.

The fifth one I didn't remember. I wouldn't have; in it I had my camera up to my face and was concentrating on lining up the perfect shot. Ben stood behind me, but he wasn't wearing the goofy smile he'd had in the other pictures. He was staring right at me with those big puppy-dog eyes, and his smile wasn't goofy at all, but . . .

"Uh-huh," Rayna said triumphantly. She had climbed onto my bed and was looking at the picture over my shoulder. "Knew that one would stop you. There is only one word for the look on that boy's face, Clea: love-struck. Which is probably why a bunch of websites are reporting he's about to propose."

"What?"

"Messenger. Don't kill the messenger."

I looked back at the picture. Ben did look love-struck. Very love-struck.

"It could just be the picture," I said. "They caught him at a weird moment."

"Yeah, a weird moment when he thought no one was looking so he showed how he really felt."

I gave Rayna back the phone and shook my head. "Ben and I are like brother and sister. That's gross."

"Hey, I read *Flowers in the Attic*. It was kind of hot."

"Shut up!" I laughed.

"I'm just saying, think about it. Really think about it. Is it that hard to believe that Ben's in love with you?"

I reflexively scrunched my face at her words—

it just seemed so weird to me. Ben and I didn't have that kind of relationship. He teased me about everything, and I gave it right back to him. That's what we were about. The picture was one thing, but Ben never looked at me like that in real life.

Or did he?

I remembered the Copacabana beach, after the Sambadrome. The way he'd held his arms around me. The way he'd looked at me after he pushed back my hair. He'd said he wanted to tell me something . . . was that it? Was he going to tell me that he was in love with me?

And if I was being honest . . . hadn't I kind of felt the same way? Maybe not in love, but I remembered being in his arms and liking the way it felt . . . and even wanting more . . .

"Oh my God, Rayna . . . I think something almost happened with Ben and me in Rio."

"What? Wait, back up. When? You mean, 'almost happened' like . . . what? What exactly almost happened?"

"I'm not sure," I said. "It all went really fast. I was feeling all these things, and he was looking at me like . . . like he was in that picture, and then . . ."

"Yeah??"

"I saw Sage."

"Ooooh." Rayna winced. "What did Ben do?"

"Nothing. I mean, I ran after Sage and . . . you know everything that happened then. We haven't even talked about it." I looked at her plaintively. "What do I do?"

"What do you want to do?"

I thought about it. "I don't know."

"Well . . . how do you feel?" she asked.

"I don't know that either. I never even thought about Ben that way except for that split second in Rio, and even then I wasn't thinking of it seriously. And Sage . . . with Sage it's *all* I think about, but it's all jumbled up with the most insane things: dreams, and other lives, and other people's memories, and . . . I don't even know what's real."

Rayna took it all in.

"I love Ben," she said. "You know that. I think you guys could be great together. I also believe in soulmates. Not just as romantic flings, like the guys in Europe, but *true* soulmates, destined to be together forever because they're perfect for each other. Are you and Sage true soulmates? I don't know, but I do know you're cheating yourself if you don't at least try to find out."

"How do I find that out, Rayna?"

"I want you to do me a favor. Promise on our friendship."

"Promise what?"

"Asking first is cheating. Promise on our friendship."

It was an evil ploy. Rayna knew I wouldn't say no, and she knew I wouldn't go back on something if I promised on our friendship. Neither of us ever would—that was a rule we'd established when we were five.

"Okay . . . I promise on our friendship," I agreed, rolling my eyes. "What did I just promise to do?"

"For the rest of the evening, *don't think*. Just listen to how you feel and go with it, wherever it leads. And whether or not it makes any sense."

I nodded. "I'll try."

"Not good enough. You promised on our friendship."

I smiled. "I'll do it."

"Perfect." She picked up the house phone and dialed. "Hey! Our room in an hour for dinner. Ask Sage what kind of pizza he likes. . . . Okay, thanks." She hung up and grabbed her purse. "Let's go."

"Where are we going?"

"We're picking up dinner. It's a crime to eat chain-restaurant pizza when we're this close to Manhattan. Come on."

I followed her, but we ended up not driving all the way into the city. The girl behind the front desk happened to be a pizza aficionado, and she knew a great little place nearby where she said we'd find pizza as good as anywhere in Manhattan. We got back to the room forty-five minutes later with three large pizzas, sodas, paper plates, cups, napkins, and an aroma that was so good it was driving me insane. I changed into comfy sweats and a T-shirt, threw my hair in a ponytail . . . then slipped into the bathroom and brushed on a quick layer of mascara.

"YES!" I cried, when the guys knocked on the door. "Finally—I'm starving!"

Rayna stopped me before I let them in.

"Remember," she whispered, "you swore on our friendship."

I nodded. Honestly, at that moment I would have sworn on our friendship to anything if it got me to the pizza sooner.

I flung open the door. "Come in and sit and tell me what kind of pizza you want before I eat it all."

The room was kind of tiny, so we sprawled out

on the beds: Rayna and me on one, Sage and Ben on the other.

"Wow, this pizza is so good," I said, swallowing a gooey bite.

"It is," Ben agreed. "But I think Sage needs a little more garlic on his. Piri says he loves the stuff."

"Nice," I said, nodding.

"So what have you guys been doing since we got to the hotel?" Rayna asked.

"Playing cribbage," Ben said. "Ask Sage who won."

"You say that like you never lost a game," Sage countered.

"Not at all. I'm just asking you to inform the ladies who won the *most* games."

"That would be you," Sage admitted.

"Four out of seven," Ben crowed, "which is like winning the Stanley Cup of cribbage."

I had no idea what that meant. Ben had to explain that the Stanley Cup is a best-of-seven match.

"I prefer soccer," Sage said. "In the World Cup the preliminary games are just lead-ups to the final. And if Ben would be so kind as to let you know who won our *final* game . . ."

"Misnomer," Ben said. "You won the last game

we played before dinner, yes, but the *final* game won't come until right before we go our separate ways. You let me know when you're about to head back to South America for good, and I'll bring out the cards for that match. I'm ready whenever you are."

He said it lightly, but his eyes were steely, and we all picked up on his real message.

Never one to let a tense moment sit, Rayna jumped in to take the reins of the conversation. She was a maestro. She knew exactly how to conduct each of us—myself included—to bring out the best: the most charming stories that showcased our most winning qualities, and got us all laughing and having fun. If a topic threatened to turn serious, Rayna breezily steered the conversation someplace lighter without it ever feeling anything but perfectly natural. I had sworn on our friendship to spend the evening *feeling*, not thinking, and if I was really focusing on my feelings, Rayna was winning my heart more than anyone.

Oops, I was already messing up. I was supposed to *not* focus. It wasn't how I normally functioned. I'd have to think like Rayna. I'd have to think logically.

Ben started to tell a story. I specifically made an

effort not to focus on it. Not that I ignored him—I watched him as he spoke, I smiled and laughed at all the right points. But I let the actual words wash over me without getting too caught up in the meaning, while I munched on my pizza and *experienced* him.

Ben had the most expressive face I'd ever seen. When he told a story, he dove into it, re-enacting each character with a new set of his jaw and cast of his brow. His eyes shone vibrantly, and every time he laughed, it showed in his whole body. Just watching him made me smile. I felt warm around him, and happy, and comfortable. I felt like flannel pajamas, hot cocoa, a teddy bear, and my favorite comedy on DVD. I felt like home.

I loved Ben, that's what I felt. It popped into my head, and I didn't doubt it for a second. I loved Ben.

Well that was settled then, wasn't it?

Then my eyes darted to Sage, and I noticed he wasn't focused on Ben's story either. He was watching me. He was watching me watch Ben, to be precise, leaning back on his elbows and staring so fixedly that I could practically hear him scratching his way into my brain to listen to what I was thinking.

And the minute I felt that, I was desperate

to take back what I'd thought, and make sure he hadn't understood. Especially since I had the strong feeling that if he believed I loved Ben, he'd disappear. Maybe not right away, but as soon as he could. And that would be the end of the world.

"Okay, Sage, your turn," Rayna said. "What's the most embarrassing thing you've ever done in the middle of a social function?"

Instantly Sage's intense stare was gone, replaced by a relaxed pose and a charming smile. "Um, I would say doing a spit take in front of Clea's mom, several senators, and the Israeli foreign minister would probably cover it."

"You did that?" I asked.

"Oh yes, he did." Rayna nodded.

"And the minister still offered you his house in Tel Aviv for the honeymoon? That's shocking."

"Rayna is particularly charming," Sage noted.

"Thank you, darling." She batted her eyes at him like a Disney princess.

"What happened?" Ben asked. "Piri spiked your drink with garlic?"

"You say that like it's a joke," Sage said. "I'm pretty sure she did."

"She must really have it out for you," Ben said.

"*Pálinka*'s Hungarian holy water. You don't mess with that."

"Speaking of holy water, I so did not get that on our trip," Rayna put in. "Clea and I were touring one of the cathedrals in Italy, and in front of the whole tour I go, 'That's so cute! Look, they have birdbaths in the church!'"

And just like that she whisked the conversation away from Ben and Sage and made everything light and frothy again. She was amazing. I grabbed another slice of pizza and sat back to enjoy the evening and see what else I'd feel.

"Movie time!" Rayna cried when we'd eaten our fill. "I checked out the pay-per-view, and we have some excellent selections. All we need are snacks." She dug into her purse and tossed me her keys. "You and Sage go. You know what Ben and I like."

"I'll go too," Ben offered.

"Are you sure?" Rayna asked. "'Cause I was really, really hoping you could help me with my AP History homework. It's a nightmare."

Oh, she was good. She looked pleadingly at Ben. He had been played by a master. If he didn't want to look like a total jerk, he had to agree.

"Okay, I'll help you," he said.

"Thank you!" she gushed. She winked at me as Sage and I headed out the door. We didn't say anything until we were in Rayna's car and driving, enveloped in the darkness of the night.

"Think Ben has any idea?" Sage asked.

I had been carrying on an intense internal monologue, trying to imagine the best way to start the right conversation, and his voice took me by surprise. "What?"

Sage smiled. "You don't think Rayna was giving us a chance to be alone?"

I turned to look at him. The light from the dashboard glowed on his face, and the knowing look in his eyes made my heart skip.

Rayna had told me to go with how I felt.

I felt like grabbing his face and kissing him.

But I couldn't. Not yet. I needed to know what he was thinking, what he felt, who he *was*. With a silent apology to Rayna, I pulled the car onto the shoulder and put it into park. The road was fairly desolate, lit only by sparse streetlamps, and the even sparser flow of other cars' headlights.

Sage looked at me, waiting.

I looked at the steering wheel.

"How does it work?" I asked, turning to face

him. "How do you know where to find me . . . us?"

Sage's eyes registered shock, but only for a moment.

"You know," he said.

I nodded.

"How?"

Everything would change once I said it out loud. Should I even do it?

"I have dreams," I admitted. "I've had them since I first saw you in the pictures. Dreams of us together . . . only it's not really us."

"No?" he asked. His voice was calm, but his hand gripped the armrest.

My heart thudded against what I wanted to say. "In the dreams I'm them. All of them: Olivia, Catherine, Anneline, Delia . . ."

I spoke gently, but it was as if I struck him with each name. His eyes shadowed. I wondered if I was making a mistake. Should I stop? I couldn't.

"I thought they were fantasies at first, but they're not. I'm dreaming in memories. Their memories. My memories."

Sage clenched his jaw. He closed his eyes and pressed his fist to his temple.

"I have these dreams," I continued, "and I feel what they felt . . . the way they felt about you.

And then I look at you, right here in front of me, and it's all there, and I want to trust it, but . . . I don't know what's real." I took a deep breath and stared at the emblem in the center of the steering wheel, so I wouldn't have to look at his reaction. "How do you feel about me?"

It sounded so stupid, but it felt monumental. I felt totally exposed.

"Clea . . . look at me," he said.

"I can't."

"Look at me."

I turned to face him.

"Why are you looking at my nose?" he asked. "My eyes, Clea."

I met his eyes. They were rich and deep, unguarded for the first time outside my dreams.

"Do you really need to ask how I feel about you?"

I didn't. I saw now that all the things I felt, he did too . . . but I was still insecure. I didn't want to push him away with all my questions, but I had to ask one more.

"Is it me, or is it them? Who do you see when you look at me?"

"I see you," he answered as if it were obvious. "It's not like I see a place, or a time, or a name:

just you. Your essence. Your soul. That's how I find you every time you come back. I know it's hard to understand, but your soul calls me . . . and I'm drawn to it. I couldn't keep away if I tried."

Sage raised his hand to my cheek, cupping it gently. I closed my eyes, resting against the warmth of his palm. When I opened them he had moved closer.

I closed the distance between us and kissed him.

I felt dizzy and hot and floaty, like every cliché . . . but it was true. I couldn't feel my feet. I finally felt like I was where my soul belonged.

There was only one problem. The gearshift was digging into my side.

"Ow!" I winced.

"You okay?"

"Yeah . . . it's just . . ." I gestured down, feeling like an idiot for ruining the moment.

Sage didn't seem to mind. He reached down and moved his seat back to its maximum leg room, then held out his hand. I grabbed it and clambered over the center console, clumsily ducking and folding myself until I finally settled onto his lap, straddling his legs. It was the least coordinated act of seduction ever.

"Better?" he asked.

"Better."

He kissed me, sliding his hands up the back of my shirt. It felt incredible. Without breaking away from his lips, I reached underneath his tee and felt his bare, sleek chest. My breath came faster, caught up in the frenzy of finally letting go and doing what I'd been dying to do from the second I'd seen Sage on the beach.

"Wait," he said.

He reached down and pulled a lever. I let out a little scream as his seat back dropped all the way and I fell on top of him. I loved the feel of his body under mine. I didn't want a single part of us *not* touching.

"Better now?" Sage murmured into my ear. It wasn't fair of him to ask me a question when he was doing that. I could barely function, never mind put together an answer.

"Much better," I said. "It's practically a bed."

"Is it?" Sage agreed, and in his eyes I saw exactly what that could mean.

"Oh," I said, suddenly nervous. "But . . . we can't. I mean, we don't have . . ."

"I do," he said, leaning down to kiss the hollow where my neck met my shoulder.

"You do?"

I tensed up. Why did he have one? For who?

The corner of Sage's mouth turned up. "For *us*, Clea. The drugstore in Rio? I kind of had a feeling. . . ."

He moved his lips back to my neck. He nibbled on my earlobe, and I whimpered.

"Oh," I managed. "Well . . . then . . ."

"I love you, Clea."

Everything tunneled in, and I heard the words echo in my head. Sage loved me. *Me*. I didn't even realize I'd stopped breathing until he said my name, concerned.

"Clea?"

I looked at him and immediately relaxed.

"I love you, too."

We kissed, and I actually felt myself melting into him as my last coherent thoughts gave way to pure sensation.

eleven

I COULDN'T wipe the smile off my face.

I felt giddy all the way back to the hotel.

I giggled.

I was happy.

Sage leaned back in his seat and studied me, an amused smile on his face.

"What?" I asked.

He shook his head.

"You're making fun of me," I said.

"I'm not," Sage assured me.

I knew he was telling the truth. His eyes were affectionate. I was his, not just in the past but today and forever, and nothing had ever made me feel more secure.

I was about to pull into the hotel when Sage reminded me of the snacks—the whole reason we'd supposedly gone out. I swung a wild U-turn that slammed Sage against his door.

"Taking up stunt driving?" he asked.

"Can you imagine walking in without the snacks? Rayna would be all over me."

"You don't think she will be anyway? It's been a long snack run."

"It hasn't been *that* long," I said. "Has it?"

He scrunched his brows. "What are you trying to say?"

I giggled again, and we pulled into a gas station market. Sage wrapped his arm around my shoulders and I leaned against his chest as we walked in step into the store; he held my hand as I cruised the tiny aisles; he stood behind me and rubbed my shoulders as we paid.

I felt normal. I imagined how things would be after everything was over: after we met the dark lady, after we got the Elixir, after we found my dad. Sage and I could travel the world together: me taking pictures, him painting, always coming back together at the end of the day to share what we'd done and lie in each other's arms.

Sure, there'd be some things to work out. Like the fact that he had eternal life and bands of psychopaths were actively tracking him down and trying to destroy him. But hey, every couple has its issues.

Then, of course, there was the very good chance that I was destined to die horribly, just like all the others.

I didn't want to think about that, though. Not tonight. Not when I was back behind the steering wheel, pretending to pay attention to the road when every bit of my concentration was on Sage's fingers entwined in my hair, playing with it gently.

I parked as far away from our rooms as I could. I didn't want Ben or Rayna to see us from the window. I turned off the car and Sage was already there, leaning over to kiss me. It was physically painful to break away, not knowing when I'd get to kiss him again.

We held hands as we walked toward the hotel, but the second the outside lights hit us, we pulled apart. We hadn't talked about it; it was just instinctual for both of us. It was better if Rayna and Ben didn't know. Especially Ben.

Even though Sage and I were apart, I felt his

hands on me. I had a feeling I always would.

"We're back!" I cried when we got back to the room.

Ben stood on alert. From his position, he looked like he'd been pacing. Rayna was sprawled on the bed, totally relaxed. A huge pile of expertly completed homework was stacked neatly on the floor.

I dumped the two bags of loot onto the bed. "We have snacks, everybody!"

"Where'd you get them from, Delaware?" Ben asked. He was glaring behind me, where Sage leaned casually against the wall.

"Practically," I said. "My fault—I was dying for Red Hots. Pretty much impossible to find. So what movie are we watching?"

Back in the cave, Sage had told me I wasn't much of an actress, and apparently he was right. I thought I put on a brilliant show, but Ben's eyes were filled with suspicion, Rayna looked like she was ready to pounce, and Sage seemed to be working very hard to stifle his laughter.

Rayna yawned. "Can't do it. I'm so tired. I'm sorry, but I have to kick you guys out and get some sleep."

She wasn't much better at acting than I was.

I knew she wanted to talk, but the idea of being away from Sage killed me.

"No worries," I said. "I can bring the snacks to the guys' room. We can watch there and let you sleep."

"Great!" Ben said.

Rayna gaped, and in the space of ten seconds, she and I had a full conversation with only our eyes.

Rayna: "What the hell?"

Me: "I know! But I want to hang out with Sage."

Rayna: "Are you insane?! You'll be with him for the rest of your life. I'm only with you until morning!"

I couldn't fight that one. She was right.

"Actually, I'm pretty tired too," I said. I even forced a yawn, though judging from Sage's smirk, it wasn't terribly convincing.

"You sure?" Ben asked. He was staring at me in a way that made me feel X-rayed.

"Positive. Take some snacks, though. I got dark chocolate M&Ms and Fritos."

"Sounds like a slumber party!" Rayna said.

"Absolutely," Sage deadpanned. "Look out, Ben—I do a mean French braid."

Ben paid no attention. He had moved closer and was looking at me suspiciously, like a dog whose owner comes home after playing with someone else's pet. I almost thought he was going to smell me.

"G'night," he said. He had to brush past Sage to get to the door, but he didn't say a word to him. Sage raised an amused eyebrow to me.

"Good night, ladies," he said, then turned and followed Ben out. It hurt to see him go, like someone had run an ice cream scoop through my core, but I knew that was melodramatic. I'd see him in the morning. We had our whole lives to be together. Tonight he could spend with Ben.

I laughed out loud, imagining the two of them actually chatting, snacking, and French braiding each other's hair as they sat cross-legged on the bed.

Then a pillow smacked me in the side of the head.

"'We can watch there and let you sleep'?" Rayna wailed. "Are you crazy?"

"I know! I'm sorry. I took it back, though, right?"

"You have two seconds to start talking, or I reload."

Before now, if anyone had told me that I could have a night like tonight and *not* want to tell Rayna everything, I'd have thought they were crazy. But being with Sage was different. It felt perfectly round and complete. If I said anything about it, I felt like I'd be giving away a giant scoop of it that I couldn't ever get back.

"It was really nice," I said. "Thanks."

Rayna picked up another pillow, then let it drop. She wasn't happy, but she understood. She also knew I wasn't thanking her just for asking, but for everything.

"Ready for bed?" she asked. "We have to beat the guys to breakfast so they don't steal all the cinnamon rolls."

I loved her like crazy.

We didn't need to leave for the airport until around eleven in the morning, but I was awake by seven. For the first time in ages, I was completely well rested, but that wasn't what had me so energized. I'd dreamed about last night with Sage—not some enhanced super version of it, but exactly the way it happened. It was perfect just the way it was.

I woke up aching to be with him, and I was so impatient about it that I couldn't even lie still. I wondered if I could knock on his door and get him without waking Ben. Could I use Rayna's phone and text him? But Ben would be just as likely to hear the phone as Sage.

This was so frustrating! Sage could be awake and feeling exactly the same way, but we had no way of letting each other know.

I needed to get up and do something. A run would be perfect. I changed and slipped down to the tiny fitness room. I pushed out five miles, totally sweating out the worst of my anxious energy.

Rayna was still asleep when I got back to the room. I showered and sneaked down to the breakfast buffet. I hoped Sage might be there waiting for me, but when I didn't see him, I grabbed a huge tray of cinnamon rolls, a coffee, and a tea, then carried them back to the room. Rayna hadn't moved. I took a cinnamon roll and waved it under her nose.

"Mmmm," she said, her eyes still closed. I waved it around some more, totally amused that I was messing with her dreams.

"AAAH!" I screamed as Rayna's head zipped forward and she chomped down on the roll.

"Excellent!" she said, sitting up. "Thanks!"

"Rayna! You almost bit my finger off!"

"You asked for it." She took another bite. "Mmmm. Oh my God, this is totally better than sex." She looked at me pointedly. "Would you agree?"

"Whoa, subtle much?"

"You don't have to talk about it if you don't want to." She knew it was the right thing to say, but her eyes were so clearly *dying* to know that I laughed out loud. I actually wanted to talk about it now, just to keep it all alive in my head.

I told her everything. Watching her reactions was like watching a silent movie: Her face registered every detail in IMAX-size emotions.

"Am I allowed to have a moment of 'ew' for my poor deflowered passenger seat?" she asked when I was finished.

I winced and buried my head in my hands. "Um . . . yeah."

"Thank you." She paused a moment, then grinned and burst out, "Clea, oh my God!!"

"I know. I know."

"So what happens now?"

"We go to Tokyo, just like we'd planned."

"What about Ben?" she asked. "Are you going to tell Ben?"

I looked at her like she was crazy.

"Hello! Not like everything you told me, just—are you going to let him know you're together?"

"I don't know," I admitted. "I don't think so. . . ."

"You really think you're going to be able to hide it?"

She had a point. I wasn't sure I'd been very good at hiding how I felt about Sage *before* last night. Did I really think I'd be better at it now?

"I guess we'll figure it out," I said.

Fifteen minutes later there was a knock on the door, and I practically fell on my head trying to get off the bed and answer it as quickly as possible.

"Graceful," Rayna said. "Deep breath. Be cool."

I sneered at her, then pulled open the door. It was Ben.

"Ready for the breakfast buffet?" he asked. "I hear there are great cinnamon rolls."

Rayna tossed the comforter over our crumb-filled tray. "Excellent! I'm dying for cinnamon rolls."

"Where's Sage?" I asked. I was trying for nonchalance, but I kept straining to look behind Ben and see if he was somewhere down the hall.

"He already went down." Ben said.

He did? I felt a pang in my stomach. He didn't want to come to the room? Wasn't he dying to see me as much as I was dying to see him?

"Everything okay?" Ben asked.

"Yeah it's good," I said. "Let's go eat."

Sage wasn't at the breakfast buffet.

Even Ben thought it was strange—Sage had said he'd be down there. Ben wasn't concerned, though. In fact, he looked a little giddy. "Maybe he decided not to come to Tokyo," he chirped. "Oh well, we'll do better with just the two of us."

I loved Ben, but he was seriously transparent.

"We need Sage to get the Elixir, though." Not that I cared about the Elixir at the moment. I was actually starting to worry. Where was Sage? Was he okay?

"He *says* we need him," Ben scoffed. "I bet the dark lady will tell us everything we need."

"Try his cell," I told Rayna.

She pulled out her phone and dialed. "No answer."

"Text him."

"Maybe he just bailed," Ben said.

Ben was just way too happy about this. I got it, but it was irritating.

"He says he'll meet us out front when it's time to go," Rayna said, reading his text.

"So he didn't go home," Ben mused. "Guess he's just unsociable."

I was about to snap at him when I realized I was being an idiot. Sage wanted to see me alone. His text to Rayna was a message to *me*.

"Excuse me," I said as I got up. "I'll be right back."

"About time," Rayna muttered. Apparently she understood the message way before I did.

I walked toward the bathrooms, then darted off to the lobby and slipped out the front door, fully expecting Sage to sweep me into his arms and kiss me.

It didn't happen. He wasn't there.

"Sage?" I called.

No answer. I walked around the outside of the hotel, but I didn't see him. I tried everywhere. I looked behind every tree, every pillar, every row of cars. I knew it was all pointless—if he'd wanted to meet me, he wouldn't be playing Super Spy, he'd be where I could see him—but I didn't want to think about the alternative.

If he wasn't waiting for me . . . he was avoiding me.

The air felt thicker and heavier.

I walked back inside to the breakfast area. Rayna caught my eye as I entered and shot me a wicked smile, but it quickly faded. I saw all my fears reflected in her face, and I couldn't take it. I veered off and shot to the bathroom.

Thank God it was empty. I grabbed the sink with both hands and steadied myself as a sob broke from inside me.

I shut my eyes and forced myself to take a deep breath. Another. I trembled, trying to hold back a fit of tears, but I couldn't let them out and go back to Ben with a red, puffy face. I looked in the mirror and stared myself down, willing myself to get a grip.

Three more deep breaths.

I ran the tap and doused my hands in freezing cold water, then held them to my face.

I was okay.

I wasn't okay at all . . . but I could keep it together.

I rejoined Ben and Rayna at the table.

"You okay, Clea?" Ben asked. "You look kind of pale."

I forced a smile. "Yeah. Too many cinnamon rolls."

"There are never too many cinnamon rolls," Rayna enthused, but it was only for Ben's benefit. She launched into some kind of conversation to keep him occupied so I could sit and think.

Why was Sage avoiding me? Did he regret what happened?

But he'd wanted it. He'd *prepared* for it.

Of course he wanted it, I imagined Rayna saying. *He's a guy.*

Okay . . . but he said he loved me. And Sage wasn't just a guy. He was my soulmate.

It sounded so lame in my head—"But he said he loved me"—like the ultimate naive-girl reaction to Mr. He's Just Not That Into You, but this was different. I wasn't being dreamy and romantic—I had *evidence*.

The three of us stayed at the breakfast buffet until we had to grab our bags and leave for the airport. When we walked out the front door, there was Sage, leaning against the outside of the hotel, his hands shoved deep into his front pockets.

He didn't even look at me.

I wanted to scream. I felt like every cell in my body was reaching out to him, desperate to get his attention, but he wouldn't even glance my way.

"Hey," he said, nodding, as he fell into step with

us, but he didn't say it to me. It was like I didn't exist for him.

"Where have you been?" Rayna asked pointedly.

"Went for a walk," he said.

I specifically went for the backseat of Rayna's car, thinking Sage might sit next to me and I could at least find some way to get his attention . . . but he grabbed the shotgun door.

"Ooh, I was hoping Ben would sit there," Rayna said. "I always get turned around going to the airport. He gives the best directions."

She was good.

"My legs are longer," Sage said. "I'm more comfortable here."

Wow. He wasn't even being subtle about it. He was going out of his way to avoid me. He settled into the seat—where he and I were just last night—and stared out the window. Incredible. He wouldn't even risk meeting my eyes in the mirror.

I felt like I was choking.

Ben looked from me to Sage and back again, and his mouth set into a straight line. I could only imagine what he was thinking. The car was way too small for all the tension inside it—I felt like it was screaming out all my secrets. I needed to get out and breathe.

Finally Rayna pulled up to the airport curb and let us out. I had been concentrating on Sage so hard the whole ride that I was shocked to see Rayna had tears in her eyes. I hugged her tightly, and when we pulled back, we didn't let go.

"Call me," she said. "Let me know you're okay . . . with everything. I'll worry, and I'm not good at worrying. I don't do it a lot."

I leaned close, touching our foreheads together and looking her straight in the eyes. "I will be fine," I said. "You will never lose me."

I didn't know if I believed it, but it was her line, and I knew she'd appreciate that I was turning it around for her. We hugged again, then she grabbed Ben's arm and whispered in his ear, "Look out for her, okay?" Ben promised he would. Rayna gave Sage a cold stare. She walked back to her car and drove away.

Inside, none of us spoke as Sage bought our tickets and we went through security, then walked to our gate. Sage sat first. I wondered if he'd actually get up and move away if I tried to sit next to him.

Ben moved close to me and lowered his voice. "Want to talk about it?"

I shook my head. "Want to go for a walk?"

"Yeah."

I wondered if Sage bothered to look at me as we walked away. I wouldn't turn back and check. It would be too awful if he didn't even care enough to look. How had everything changed so much in just one night?

Ben waited until we'd put some distance behind us before he spoke.

"I totally respect that you don't want to talk about it. You don't have to. At all. I just want to know . . . did he hurt you?"

"Ben . . ."

"Just tell me—did he hurt you?" The words scratched out of Ben's throat. I realized his whole body had tensed, and his hands had balled into fists.

Yes, he did. Horribly. In this life and probably all the others.

"No," I said. "He didn't. I'm fine. I promise."

It was the biggest lie I could possibly ever tell. I sold it hard. I even smiled and squeezed Ben's hand to prove it was true.

In a long breath, Ben let out all his tension. "Okay, good."

How had I ever doubted that Ben loved me? It seemed so obvious now. I wondered if things would have been different if I'd known it a year ago, before I ever saw Sage. If I'd spent a year loving Ben, would the pictures of Sage have had the same effect on me? Would I have even noticed him? Would he have even *been* in the pictures, or would he have dissolved away, our connection broken because I'd found someone else?

I could make that choice now, I realized. I could block out every memory of the seismic activity Sage inspired in me and instead commit to concentrating on everything sweet, easy, and wonderful I felt about Ben. Even if I didn't love Ben quite in the same way he loved me, I did love him. Wasn't that enough? Ben would never torture me the way Sage was. He'd be good to me forever. All I'd have to do was kiss him, right now.

I imagined myself doing it. Standing on tiptoe, wrapping my arms around his neck as I tilted my lips to his, and with that single kiss promising to be as faithful to him as he always had been to me, no matter what else happened.

Instead I checked my watch. "We still have lots of time. Want to get some magazines?"

"How about I buy you a coffee? I saw a store with a gingerbread mocha. You love ginger—you'll go crazy for it."

"Never going to happen, Ben. Never," I lilted

as I walked off, officially stepping away from the rapids and back into the simple currents of our friendship.

Sage still hadn't moved by the time we got back to the gate. He didn't look up, either.

I felt a small flicker of anger leap into my chest.

Yes. That was better. That made me feel stronger.

How dare he? After what we did last night, how the hell dare he?

If he was my soulmate, my soul needed to develop better taste.

I strode toward him and sat next to him. He didn't get up and leave. He also didn't look my way.

I wasn't letting him get away with it anymore.

"Look at me, Sage."

I saw his jaw muscle working. He didn't move.

"Into my eyes. Look at me."

He did. As always, I saw the truth there. His feelings hadn't changed from last night, but something had.

"Don't play games with me. I deserve better than that. If you want to leave me, just *leave*. I don't need you to find the Elixir or my dad."

"I'm leaving the minute I can."

That was it. He wasn't even going to try and explain. I felt devastated inside, like the silent aftermath of a massive hurricane.

Fine. I wasn't going to beg. He could leave whenever he wanted. I was done.

An hour later we were in the air, Sage across the aisle from Ben and me. Ben offered a cribbage game. I wasn't in the mood. I willed myself not to think about Sage. I flipped through a magazine, I watched a movie for a bit . . . and finally I fell asleep.

This time I didn't dream about Sage. I dreamed about my father. It was such a simple dream. Dad, Mom, and I back home doing nothing of any consequence: eating dinner together and teasing Mom for going on one of her random and bizarre homemade cooking jags; Dad bent over the Saturday *New York Times* crossword puzzle—much harder than Sunday's—and recruiting Mom's and my help; all of us cuddled up and watching TV together: Dad with his arm around Mom, me sprawled out across the couch, wrapped in an afghan, my head resting on Dad's leg. Dad looked a little older, a little thinner, but he was fine. He was there. The whole year he'd been missing was a distant memory now, something we didn't dwell on because we'd moved so completely past it.

It didn't feel like a dream, it felt like a premonition. I woke up many hours later, just in time for our descent into Tokyo. The dream and the long sleep energized me. I felt hopeful. Optimism and drive surged through me like a shot of straight caffeine. I was suddenly sure we could succeed, but only if we worked together. That meant Sage too, and he couldn't help if he and I weren't speaking.

My feelings didn't matter right now. After we found the dark lady, after we found the Elixir, after we found my father, *then* I could deal with Sage rejecting me. Until then I didn't have the luxury of being heartbroken.

I surprised both Sage and Ben with my upbeat small talk as we trekked through the airport, waited for the bus, then took the long ride to Shibuya station. I don't think either of them expected me to sound so positive and chipper. That was my new attitude though—anything to make the team work.

We stopped at a hotel in Shibuya and got a couple of rooms. We hoped to find Magda right away, but in case we didn't, we needed a place to stay. We also wanted to drop off our bags. We did everything as quickly as we could, but it was still past sundown by the time we emerged onto the street.

Shibuya felt like Times Square, crammed with towering buildings, each covered in blinking lights and shining neon signs and constantly changing video billboards that threatened to overload the senses. Cars whizzed by in a constant stream, their headlights adding to the visual blur.

We saw it right away: the soaring cylinder of Shibuya's top fashion store, its electric pink 109 blazing through the night sky. It seemed like the least likely place to find the key to an ancient mystery, and for just a moment I wondered if we could have possibly misunderstood my dad's messages.

No. They were clear. As incongruous as it seemed, we were in the right place.

When we were just across the street from it, I turned to Sage. "Have you ever been to this part of Tokyo?" I asked.

"A couple times."

"This is my favorite part."

That was when the traffic lights changed and all the cars stopped, in every direction. Pedestrians flooded the intersection, filling crosswalks that ran every which way. We joined the mad scramble, walking among throngs of tourists from all over the world mixed with Japan's hippest scenesters, all crammed into the street and lit by the waiting headlights of cars, cabs, and buses.

As we maneuvered through the crowds, I noticed people looking at us. It was weird. Young, giggling fashionistas weren't the type who usually recognized me, but today they did. Pairs and groups of Japanese girls did double takes as we passed them, their eyes going wide as they clutched one another's arms and waved their hands in front of their mouths, whispering and giggling. Some even snapped pictures with their wildly decorated cell phones.

"Ho-ly crap," Ben said, and I followed his open-mouthed stare upward to the giant screen on the side of the QFront Building. It was airing some gossipy entertainment show . . . featuring the pictures of Ben and me at Carnival. Right now the one of him staring at me while I shot pictures of the Samba Parade was up, and while I couldn't read Japanese, it wasn't hard to imagine what the swirly pink script accented with hearts and flowers implied.

Not that the look on his face needed any added explanation.

A deafening sea of horns spurred us across the street, and we just made it to the curb before all Shibuya Crossing again flooded with traffic.

"Wow, um, that's . . . um . . ." Ben couldn't even finish his sentence.

"It's trouble." Sage sounded irritated. He nodded to another girl snapping my picture. "You don't think that's going up on the web?"

I winced. He was right—we had a far bigger problem than Ben or me feeling embarrassed. We had worked so hard to remain off the grid, and now countless people had probably Tweeted and Facebooked my image all over the world. If Cursed Vengeance or the Saviors of Eternal Life were scanning the Internet and looking for me, they'd be rewarded soon enough.

The Saviors of Eternal Life web forum I'd seen in Dad's studio flashed into my mind. Should we check it to see if we'd been spotted?

No, it wasn't like it was comprehensive—it wouldn't tell us anything for certain. It would be a waste of time.

What we *could* do was get a little less conspicuous. After all, we were at the mall.

We went inside Shibuya 109. Japanese pop music rang in our ears, and the hottest fashions leaped out of each crammed storefront. Every inch of its ten floors was packed with shoppers. Rayna would have gone nuts. She'd at least appreciate it if I did a little shopping while I was here.

I asked Sage for the credit card, then ducked into the first store I saw that looked right. It took no time at all to grab a short black wig, large sunglasses, a pair of ripped jeans, and a tank top.

I changed in the fitting room, then stepped out to find Ben at the entrance of another store, confused and transfixed by a pink Hello Kitty cell phone case absolutely covered in Swarovski crystals. As I watched him, he turned it curiously, then pressed a button on the side of the case. The crystal kitty head popped up to reveal a hidden compact mirror.

"I think it's you," I chirped.

Ben wheeled around and smiled approvingly. "I like it. Very Japanese."

"Thank you," I said. "I also got something for you."

"I'm not wearing a wig."

"You're such a downer." I handed him a baseball cap, then took off my camera case and slung it around his neck. "There: Generic American Tourist. No one will look twice at you."

"I'll choose not to take that as an insult."

"You look fine," Sage said, all business. "Let's find The Little Door."

I checked the directory. "Sixth floor."

We raced upstairs to the store and asked for Magda Alessandri. We knew she might not be working this shift, but figured we could at least nail down when we might find her.

But no one by that name worked in the store. On any shift.

"So if she's not here . . . where is she?" Ben asked.

Neither Sage nor I had an answer.

"Okay . . . maybe I was being too literal," I said. "Maybe Dad's note didn't mean the *store* The Little Door. Maybe we're supposed to be looking for an actual little door."

I would be the first to admit that it sounded odd, but I wasn't sure what else to try.

"So . . . we just search the entire mall looking for particularly tiny doors?" Sage asked drily.

"I'm totally open to other ideas if you have them," I said.

Neither of them had another idea. We decided

to be methodical: The cylindrical mall had ten stories, two of them below ground level, so our smartest move felt like heading downstairs and working our way up, looking into each store for anything that might qualify as a "little door," then asking at those places for Magda. It was incredibly daunting, and it could take an insanely long time—far too long if the wrong people had seen us on the Web and were coming after us—but we didn't see another way.

We found very few little doors, and no Magdas at any of them. By the time we got to the top floor, we moved slowly, none of us wanting to believe the truth.

We had failed.

"Maybe Grant wrote the wrong coordinates on the board," Ben finally said.

"He wouldn't do that," I argued. "If he went out of his way to etch tiny numbers inside a cribbage board, he'd be careful enough not to get them wrong."

"We've been through everything here," Sage said. "Your father must have made a mistake."

"Stop saying that! It's not possible!" I insisted. "I can't believe you're both ready to give up!"

"It's not giving up," Ben said. "It's just . . ." He let

the sentence trail off, which said it all. He thought it was hopeless. Sage looked like he agreed.

"You're both wrong," I said. "We must have missed something. We'll come back tomorrow. And the next day if we have to. Maybe we spoke to the wrong people—people who don't know Magda."

Neither Ben nor Sage answered, and neither of them would look me in the eye. They both knew we had a limited amount of time in Shibuya. We couldn't avoid the people chasing us forever.

Then Ben tilted his head, as if curious. He wandered away from Sage and me, down a hall. We'd seen it already—there wasn't much there except bathrooms and the elevator.

"Clea! Sage!" Ben called, and we joined him.

"We've been so sure the little door is in one of the stores, but what if it isn't? What if it's tucked away somewhere?"

Ben nodded to the door in front of him. It was a regular-size door labeled STAIRS in Japanese and English.

"In a back stairwell?" Sage asked.

"I guess it's possible," I said, "but how would a little door there get us to Magda Alessandri?"

"Maybe it doesn't take us to her directly," Ben

said. "Maybe it's where we get another clue that'll help us find her."

I nodded. It was frustrating to imagine yet another step before we found the dark lady, but at least Ben's idea offered hope.

"Let's look," I said.

We opened the door and started down the staircase. The public rarely used this route. It was stark, and our footsteps echoed as we followed it down and down, floor after floor, until we reached B1, the top basement level.

Nothing.

"Clea—," Sage began, but I cut him off.

"Not yet. We're not done yet."

"You're right," Ben said, and there was awe in his voice. "Look."

We'd reached a landing between the two basement floors . . . and there was a perfect little door at chest level on the wall.

"Unbelievable," I breathed. I reached out, turned the knob, and opened the door . . . to reveal a long hall, dimly lit by bare, low-wattage bulbs. I hoisted myself up and climbed inside the tiny entryway.

Once through the door, the hall was tall enough to walk through easily, though everything was disconcertingly dim. We could see exposed insulation and metal beams, but not much else. No matter how softly we walked, our footsteps seemed to scream off the walls.

The light grew brighter up ahead, and all three of us moved toward it, huddling close together as we walked farther and farther away from the door and the outside world. Finally we reached the source of the light: a tiny, cramped room, every inch of which was packed with vases, tapestries, and strange, curious antiquities. A standing golden birdcage leaned over a low carved wooden pew, which rested under a huge mirror with a frame of black wrought-iron wilted roses. Shelves teemed with dark Fabergé eggs, carved nesting dolls painted like wild animals, ancient goblets and tureens tarnished and worn . . . everything dark, old, and mysterious in a way that made my stomach roil. The stench of the room didn't help: It was musty and dank.

We tiptoed in and peered around, but saw no one at all.

I heard a creak and jumped, only to come face-to-face with an openmouthed stuffed bobcat, teeth bared for attack. I gasped.

Sage put a hand on my arm. I felt like it was the first time he'd touched me in years.

"It's okay." He took his hand off my skin, and I missed it immediately. He reached up and gently touched the bobcat's incisors.

"Sharp," he noted, "but harmless."

The three of us walked farther in. What were we looking for? Off to the side I noticed some ornate red netting, inlaid with beads. It was pretty. It blocked off another part of the room. Curious, I walked over and pulled it back . . . and started screaming hysterically.

Right in front of me, only inches away, a *human body* sat on an old velvet couch. It was the worst thing I had ever seen. It looked like a mummy without its wrapping. The tissue-thin skin had sunken to a speckled gray sheet that clung to its wasted body, falling into every crevice between each bone. The ghost of parchment lips peeled back from yellow teeth, and long, stringy strands of white hair snaked over its withered skull.

At the sound of my shrieks, its eyes popped open.

I lurched back, gasping, and slammed into Ben and Sage as the milky orbs rolled around in their sockets, taking us all in, then came to rest on my face.

And I was out.

twelve

I FOUGHT the urge to wake back up. I didn't want to see what I would see. Was that thing real?

"Your fiancée is very rude, Sage." The voice was gravelly, and thick with the grave. "Get her up and make a proper introduction."

It *was* real. And it was talking. I so did not want to open my eyes.

"Clea?"

It was Sage, and he was close. I opened my eyes and saw him leaning over me, his face filled with concern. I almost smiled. If nothing else, the horror show seemed to have brought him back to me, at least for the moment.

"Are you okay?" he asked.

Okay? I wanted to laugh, but I had a horrible feeling that if I started, it would turn into a screeching cackle of insanity I could never stop.

It was better not to trust my voice just yet. I nodded and let Sage help me to my feet. I kept my eyes glued to his face.

A dry cluck of disapproval came from the talking corpse. "Not even looking at your hostess. What Sage saw in you, Olivia, I'll never know."

The name shocked me so much that I snapped my head around to look at the thing.

A choking wheeze hacked from its chest, and it took me several moments before I realized it was laughing.

"You're surprised I know your real name," it said. "You shouldn't be. We go way back. Not as far back as your fiancé and I, of course."

The creature's eyes leered in Sage's direction. He winced.

"I also know your friend, Giovanni," it said, and rolled its eyes to Ben. He was pale and trembling. Sweat beaded down his face. He was coming completely unglued.

"Giovanni?" Sage asked. "No . . ."

"Oh, it's him," the corpse said. "You just don't see it, not the way you do with *her*. But it's him." It toyed with Ben, wiggling an impossibly bony finger toward him. It gave a wet laugh as he shied away.

"Leave them alone, Magda," Sage said.

Magda? *This* was Magda?

"But Sage, you came to me!" she said.

"You're Magda . . . *Alessandri*?" I asked, piecing together the impossible. "*You're* Shakespeare's Dark Lady?"

Her eyes narrowed to slits. "What—you can't see me as a raven-haired vixen? I was beautiful five hundred years ago. Your fiancé thought I was. He couldn't keep his hands off me."

I felt nauseous. I wasn't jealous, even though Magda clearly wanted me to be. I just kept thinking of Sage touching this woman as she was now. The image made me sick.

"F-five h-hundred years ago?" Ben stammered. "But I thought the Elixir—" He stopped cold as Magda fixed him with a glare.

"Kept one young," she finished icily. "Obviously, I didn't drink the Elixir of Life. My longevity comes from an enchantment made by my mother, a powerful mystic, the day I was born. She died in childbirth, just after sealing my life force in the glass charm I wear around my neck. As long as it remains intact, I survive."

I looked down at her sunken chest. Sure enough, a delicate glass ball dangled there from a thin chain.

Magda gave a phlegmy bark. "Had my mother survived, I'd have asked her to change the spell. Eternal life is useless without eternal youth. I can't even show my face in public anymore. I hide away here with all my belongings."

"In . . . the mall?" I asked.

"Why not? I have everything I need. A caretaker brings me anything else. And I can hear the roar of life just beyond my walls. When I close my eyes, I can almost pretend I'm still a part of it."

"But after the attack . . . I saw you dead," Sage objected.

"You saw me *playing* dead," Magda clarified. "I was stabbed seven times, you know. One dagger went clean through my stomach and out my back, pinning me to the floor. I had to lie there like a writhing, stuck bug—"

"You don't have to describe it," Sage said tightly.

"No, I do," Magda said, her eyes strong and piercing, "because it was all your fault. You knew the rules. You ignored them. And all of us paid the price."

Her words seemed to slice into Sage, and it was a moment before he could speak. "I know," he said. "Your faces have haunted me every single night. But you're not the only one who paid for it. If you've stayed alive to make sure I've suffered, I assure you, I have."

"I *have* stayed alive to see you suffer," Magda said. "I was able to do it. As head of the Society, I was closest to the Elixir. It tied you and I together. I've seen everything."

"Then you know," Sage said through gritted teeth, "I've spent centuries in a more bitter hell than anyone who died that day. I would gladly trade places with any of them."

"It's not enough. While the rest of the Society lost their lives and I turned into this withered shell, you've had happiness beyond anything we can know." She glared at me, and her papery lips managed to curl into a sneer. "You're having it still. I want more from you, but I had to wait until you came to me to get it."

Sage flinched, his eyes darting to Ben and me

before he looked back at Magda. "I'm ready. We should speak alone."

"What?" I asked. "What are you talking about?"

"I think you and Ben should go," Sage said.

"No! I'm not going anywhere. Are you insane? After we came all the way here, you really think we're going to leave? We still don't know anything!"

"The girl is right," Magda agreed. "She doesn't know anything. And I think it's time she knew *everything*." Her eyes lolled toward Ben. "I think it's time you both did."

"Magda . . . ," Sage warned.

She ignored him. "Pull up chairs. You'll want to be comfortable for this."

"No," Sage demanded, then fixed his eyes on Ben and me. "You don't have to listen to her."

"They do if they want to know about the girl's father," Magda countered. "And you won't get what you need unless you do what I say."

Sage's nostrils flared, and he pursed his lips. Then he grabbed three cushioned stools and thrust them down in front of Magda, who smiled. We sat, and she held out her hands. "Circle of hands," she said.

My stool sat between Ben's and Magda's. I

couldn't believe I had to touch her, but I didn't want to give her the satisfaction of seeing how much it bothered me. Her hand felt like crepe paper wrapped over toothpicks. I was sure the least bit of pressure would crush it to dust.

My other hand squeezed Ben's, and he and Sage completed the circle back to Magda. Magda leaned back, and her eyes closed. Suddenly her whole body convulsed. My own eyelids slammed closed like shutters. I tried to open them, but it was impossible. I was sealed inside with whatever Magda wanted to show us.

I saw Sage. He was dressed the way he was in my dreams about Olivia. He jingled gold coins in a money pouch as he walked. It was surreal. I didn't actually hear his thoughts, but I understood them. I could feel the pride he took in both his impeccable dress and his staggering family wealth. He was twenty-one years old and felt like the entire world was his for the taking.

As he climbed a set of stairs and knocked on an ornately decorated door, he sighed, and I understood that this was where he visited the Society, the group he'd complained to me about in my dream. The one he attended only to please his father.

Suddenly that image disappeared, replaced by Sage standing hand in hand with nine other men and women. They stood in a circle, and everything about their surroundings—their clothing, the furnishings in the room—pointed to incredible wealth and luxury. In the middle of the circle stood a small bejeweled curio cabinet.

I recognized Magda in the group—or rather, I knew it was her somehow, as she looked nothing like the emaciated skeleton she was now. She was the picture of vibrant youth and beauty. She gave Sage a suggestive wink, and I actually did feel a tinge of jealousy run through me. Magda's voice rang out loud and clear as she began a ceremony with the Society's vow of secrecy, then continued, "We come together to praise and protect the Elixir of Life. . . ."

But as she spoke, the scene faded away, replaced by Sage and a friend in a tavern, laughing over drinks.

I gasped out loud.

The friend was Ben.

He *wasn't* Ben, of course. He was Giovanni, whom I knew from my dreams, but suddenly, seeing him in Magda's vision, I didn't have a single doubt that *this was him*. And from the way Ben's hand suddenly went clammy as it gripped mine tightly, I was sure he knew it too.

Again, I automatically understood things I had no way of knowing. Giovanni was a shopkeeper's son, from a much lower class than Sage, though the two had known each other since childhood. Giovanni's class and financial status didn't matter to Sage at all. Giovanni was his best friend, simple as that. He loved Sage just as much, but he was acutely aware of the social gulf between them. It ate him up inside. In his worst moments, he believed their friendship was nothing more than an act of charity on Sage's part—something Sage could brag about with his rich "real" friends so he felt like a bigger man.

Sage never suspected Giovanni's darker thoughts and insecurities, so Sage had no idea what he was doing when he scoffed and laughed about the Society.

"Honestly, Gi, it's absurd. The money is dripping off the walls of this place, but none of it is anything compared to the cabinet for the great 'Elixir of Life'! Solid gold, encrusted with rubies, diamonds, emeralds . . . any gem you can imagine, it's on this cabinet. But *inside* the cabinet . . . oh, that's even better."

"What is it?" Giovanni asked, secretly salivating over the idea of the bejeweled cabinet. He imagined prying off just one or two of its perfect gems. He could feed and clothe his three little sisters for weeks. Or better, he could buy himself something fancy—a nice outfit like the kind Sage wore. Something that would make him look like a real nobleman.

"*Inside* the cabinet," Sage went on, "are three vials, each as tall as the length of my forearm, and each of which puts the cabinet to shame. More jewels, more gold, crystal stoppers . . . and all for what?"

"The Elixir of Life," Giovanni marveled. "Does it really give eternal life?"

"Come on, Gi, of course not! It can't! There's no such thing! It's just an excuse for these people to make themselves feel special—the 'Keepers of the Elixir.' It kills me that I have to spend time with those puffed-up fools."

Sage leaned back in his seat and called for the bartender to bring them another round. He had vented about the Society and was finished with it, but I could see that Giovanni's mind still chewed over everything he'd just heard.

Again the scene changed. Now Giovanni stood

in an unpaved street in a seamier part of town. With him was a gang of three boys, none of them older than nineteen. I knew—though again I had no way of knowing—that these boys had grown up in the same neighborhood as Giovanni. I also knew they were mean. Seeing them in my mind's eye, I felt a rush of evil so palpable, I wanted to open my eyes and get away. I tried, and shivered as I realized I couldn't. As long as I was in Magda's circle of hands, I didn't have control anymore—she did.

Giovanni didn't see the evil in his friends. These were his neighborhood's "cool kids," and he ached to prove he was as tough as they were. He told them Sage's story about the Society and all its riches, then puffed out his chest and added, "I'm thinking I'll bust in there sometime and nip a few things for myself." It wasn't true, but he figured it would impress them. "Maybe I'll steal the Elixir of Life vials. I bet I'd be set for good with just one of those."

"'Elixir of Life?'" the toughest of the three boys asked. "What's that?"

Giovanni explained, his attitude as scoffing as Sage's had been, but he had no idea of the spark he was lighting. Unfathomable riches *and* eternal life? Giovanni had inspired the guys to achieve their greatest haul ever. They pumped him for as many details as possible, and Giovanni blossomed under the attention, never guessing their real motives. He walked off feeling proud that the guys now saw him as *somebody*; the guys walked off determined that tomorrow would be the day *they* attacked the Society.

Immediately the scene changed again, and I saw myself.

Olivia and Sage walked arm in arm down the street in the moonlight. Ben gasped, and I knew he understood that Olivia was me. She didn't look exactly like me. This wasn't like the dreams where I saw myself as each of the other women. She looked like herself—the way Sage had drawn her on the cave floor. The way she looked in his paintings.

"Is this a big deal, presenting your bride-to-be to the Society members tonight?" Olivia teased.

"It's a big deal to be with you." Sage grinned. "You know how I feel about the Society. Their blessing is a necessary evil for my share of the family fortune."

"What makes you think we'll get their blessing? Your ex-girlfriend hates me, and she's the one who runs it."

"Magda doesn't hate you."

"Are you kidding? Have you seen the way she looks at me?"

"She might be a little jealous," Sage admitted.

"Of course! She's gorgeous! A woman like her can't possibly lose men very often. I'm sure she's just waiting for you to realize your mistake and go back to her."

"Promise me you don't really think that'll happen."

"I don't know. . . ." Olivia hedged, not meeting his eye. "She's rich and beautiful and in the Society. . . . I'm sure your father would love it if you married her."

"Are you jealous?" Sage teased.

"I don't know about *jealous*. I'm just saying—"

Sage laughed out loud and swept Olivia into his arms. "Olivia, the minute we met, other women ceased to exist. You are my soulmate. I'm not going back to anyone else. You're stuck with me forever. Deal with it."

Olivia smiled. "Okay . . . if I have to."

Sage kissed her, then held her close as they continued walking along the street.

"You have nothing to worry about from Magda," he assured her. "She can't come between us, and no matter how she feels, she'd never let it get in the way of Society business. We'll get their blessing."

"Okay, good. I have to admit, I'm so curious to see how everything works."

"Oh, I think you'll be highly amused."

The couple couldn't be more casual as they walked off, but I suddenly felt cold with terror. The truth hit me like a head-on crash.

Sage was bringing Olivia to the Society tonight.

Tonight was the night Giovanni's friends were going to strike.

No one but Sage and Magda was going to survive the attack.

I was about to watch the attack I'd envisioned in my dreams, and seen on Sage's canvases.

My heart started thumping so hard it hurt. I was about to witness my own death.

I saw the Society again circling the bejeweled cabinet, this time with Olivia standing among them. Magda led the opening chant, sneering as her eyes met Olivia's.

Suddenly the door burst open and Giovanni's pack of "friends" poured in . . . but they weren't alone. Their ranks had swelled to eight members, all armed with makeshift clubs and shivs. The luxury of the room reflected in their eyes, making them salivate with bloodthirsty greed.

"No screaming!" roared the leader, grabbing Magda and holding a roughly serrated knife to her throat. "Not a sound or she dies!"

The Society members immediately froze, and quieted into fearful whimpering. Even Sage stood still, but he wasn't giving in. He cast a sidelong glance at Olivia and nodded slightly, letting her know he had this under control. He was biding his time and waiting for the right moment.

The leader grinned at the curio cabinet. "There it is, boys," he said. "The Elixir of Life is in there. Just like Gi said."

"Gi?" Sage asked, shocked. He looked at Olivia and she shook her head in disbelief—Giovanni couldn't be responsible for this.

"Yeah, Gi, your charity case," the leader spat at Sage. "You thought he was too poor and daft to be a threat, right? But he laughs at you—comes to us and tells us everything. And now what's yours is going to be ours. *Everything* that's yours."

The leader grinned and ran his dirty fingers down Olivia's cheek. With an animal roar, Sage lunged . . . but the leader urged on two of his men. They fell on Sage, stabbing him mercilessly in his chest, in his arms, in his legs.

Olivia's sanity snapped, and she started screaming, loud and shrill. The leader warned her to stop, to close her mouth or else, but she couldn't hear. She could only scream and scream and scream. . . .

An attacker smashed a club into the back of her skull, shutting her up. It was the last thing Sage saw before he lost consciousness.

The group of attackers gathered up all the gold and jewels they could find. They wanted to move quickly and get out. They didn't even notice when Sage came to. He was on his side, barely able to pry his eyes open. Just the effort ripped his insides apart.

In the vision, I saw the room as he did. It was a slaughterhouse.

All around him lay the ripped, gashed, and blood-soaked bodies of the Society members. Magda was among them. I understood why Sage couldn't believe she had survived. She looked just the way she had described, struggling weakly against her gaping wounds and the bloody dagger pinning her to the floor.

Sage looked away. Agonized, he struggled to scan the rest of the room. Where was Olivia?

Finally he saw her. She lay sprawled on the

ground, her unseeing eyes still reflecting the shock and terror of her final moments.

I couldn't breathe. This was impossibly awful, worse than Sage's painting. This was real. And it was me. I had lived that life, and I had died that death. I was staring at the very end of me. It was too much. I began to hyperventilate. The images behind my closed eyes began to blur, and I was sure I would pass out.

Magda's weightless, skeletal hand squeezed my own—hard—forcing me back to my senses.

The vision went on.

Sage cried out in agony when he saw Olivia, but his lungs were punctured. No sound emerged. Everything inside him was broken; he knew he was about to die. He took small solace in that.

His fault . . . he had told the Society's secrets and this was what happened . . . all his fault . . .

Those would be his last thoughts, he imagined. Good. It was a message he'd take with him down to hell and deliver to the devil himself, so he could be properly punished for all eternity.

But hell wasn't a place he'd see Olivia. He had to say his final good-byes to her right now. With herculean effort, he dragged himself across the floor until he was only inches away from her face.

His strength was fading fast; there wasn't much time. He made a final lurch, but never made it. Harsh hands grabbed him, and a jeering voice shouted, "Look at this, boys! He's alive! Should I finish him off?"

"No!" said the leader. "I have a better idea."

His plan was to test the Elixir on Sage, to make sure it was real and not some kind of poisonous trick. They forced an entire vial of it down his ruined throat, then bundled him into a carriage and fled out of town.

They almost didn't make it.

The Elixir's healing powers were amazing. They couldn't save Sage from the terrible pain of his wounds, but within an hour the pain had faded, and his strength had begun to return.

Had he been more patient, things might have turned out differently. But the men in the carriage with Sage had killed Olivia. There was no hope for patience, only revenge. The second he could, Sage lunged for the nearest man, wrapping his hands around his throat and squeezing his windpipe.

The other men in the carriage were so shocked by Sage's impossible recovery that they almost didn't move in time. Finally they returned to their senses and grabbed Sage, pulling him from their friend and beating and stabbing him until he again fell into unconsciousness.

He woke faster this time, but his wrists and ankles were already tightly bound to each other behind his back. The attackers took no more chances—if Sage struggled the littlest bit, they ferociously let loose with their weapons.

Later, hiding out at an abandoned farm, the gang of attackers worked out their next steps. The murder of so many wealthy Romans wouldn't go unnoticed. The plan was for the attackers to split up with their newfound riches and fan out over Europe, once the fervor to find them had died down.

The only hitch in their plans was what to do with the Elixir . . . and with Sage. It seemed clear by now that the Elixir wasn't a hoax. They really *had* given Sage eternal life, and they all wanted the same for themselves. But was that even possible? Sage had downed an entire vial. That one was gone—the empty vessel had been lost in the scramble to get out of the house.

Two vials were left . . . but if it took an entire vial to achieve eternal life, only two of them could have it. It was possible less was needed . . . but what if they split the rest of the Elixir eight ways and it wasn't enough to give eternal life to any of them?

The gang agreed that no one would touch the Elixir until they reached a consensus, but the problem was, none of them trusted one another. They fought constantly, and watched each other so carefully, they barely slept. Those who did sleep jockeyed subtly for spots closest to the Elixir, so they'd be sure to wake up the second anyone tried to move the vials.

The situation left the gang tired, angry, and frustrated, and they took their emotions out on Sage. If they were really going to drink the Elixir, they reasoned, it only made sense to test how well it worked. After drinking a whole vial, would Sage really live through *anything,* or were some things too dramatic for even the Elixir to fix?

It was quite an outlet for them, coming up with new and creative ways to kill Sage. It also removed Sage as a threat, since each torture left him so weak that he couldn't possibly attack them again. They threw Sage off cliffs, they tied him to rocks and let wild animals attack him, they lit him on fire. Sage always recovered, but the pain was so incomprehensibly horrible that he prayed for the mercy of death.

Then he heard the gang plotting their next test: dismemberment.

Sage didn't know for sure, but he had a feeling about what would happen. He wouldn't die, but he wouldn't magically reassemble himself either. He'd live, his consciousness somehow split into whatever random pieces the captors carved him into.

He had to escape. Immediately. Despite the tightly bound restraints they kept around him, he had to find a way.

He saw his chance one night. It was very late. Five of the bleary-eyed gang were still awake, all of them armed, all vigilantly watching one another to make sure no one tried to steal the Elixir for himself. Three men stood far from Sage. Two huddled closer, plotting wild schemes to grab the Elixir and split it between them.

Yes. This would be perfect.

Sage got the attention of the closer two men. He spoke quietly, so the others wouldn't hear. He offered them a deal. If they released him, Sage would swear allegiance to them. He would help them go after the others, and make sure only *they* received the Elixir.

"Why should we believe you?" one asked.

"Yeah—what if we untie you and you come after us?"

"Why?" Sage countered. "I do that, you scream, and everyone comes after me. I wouldn't have a chance. I don't want to be tortured anymore. I need your help. If I have to help you to get it, so be it."

The two men looked at each other, clearly tempted. If Sage wiped out the others, not only would the two of them get the Elixir, but they'd also get to split all the stolen riches.

"Okay," the first man whispered. "We'll do it."

Swiftly and silently, one cut loose the ropes ensnaring Sage, while the other kept watch to make sure no one else noticed.

"There," the man said when he'd sliced Sage free. "Now you go after the others. We'll grab the Elixir."

Sage didn't answer. Instead, in one fluid movement, he whisked the knife out of the man's belt and sliced the throats of both his co-conspirators. They were dead before they realized what was happening.

The sound of the bodies hitting the ground got the attention of the men who were farther away. When they realized what had happened, their shouts woke the others. They were closer, and raced toward Sage, ready to attack.

Sage welcomed the challenge. He let his rage boil through him. He could dominate an army now; three men were nothing. He brandished the knives of both his victims, and screamed as he ran to meet his attackers. He didn't even notice the few blows they landed, but his daggers hit their marks again and again and again. He reveled in their blood.

The remaining three attackers—the friends Giovanni had first told about the Elixir—weren't stupid. They saw how the battle was going. The odds were *not* in their favor. While Sage was still occupied with the others, they quickly gathered as much of the stolen riches as they could carry and took off in the carriage.

Sage was still locked in battle, on fire with adrenaline and laughing maniacally as he unleashed his fury. He didn't even notice the three men racing away.

"Those men survived," Magda's voice croaked, narrating over her vision, "but they lived cursed lives, as has every one of their descendants throughout the centuries. Those descendants, now spread throughout the world, have become

Cursed Vengeance. The Saviors of Eternal Life are the descendents of the Society members—husbands, wives, and children who passed stories about the Elixir from generation to generation."

I heard Magda's voice, but my attention was still glued to the image in front of me. Sage stood like a wild animal among the corpses of the five men he'd killed. His blood-splattered body heaved as he tried to catch his breath. The job was done, and now, all alone, in the middle of nowhere with the rest of eternity stretching out before him, Sage's soul snapped. He dropped to his knees and screamed.

The image changed. It was later that day. I saw Sage pour out the remaining Elixir, destroying it. He buried the two vials in the dirt . . . where my father's team would dig them up centuries later.

Next I saw Sage back in Rome, his head bowed in front of Olivia's tombstone. An older man placed a hand on Sage's shoulder. It was Olivia's father. I searched the image, wondering if my father had been this man, but I didn't feel anyone familiar there. Sage was surprised to see the man, but he looked at Sage kindly, and pressed something into his palm: Olivia's iris charm necklace.

When the image changed again, Sage was smiling. He rode a horse across what I immediately understood was the English countryside in the late seventeenth century. Though his eyes still held depths of misery, he seemed happy, and I soon understood why. He was with Catherine, her red hair loose and wild as they galloped together.

Catherine and Sage lounged by a stream as their horses drank and recovered their breath. Sage reached down to touch the iris charm around her neck. "It always amazes me," he said. "I can't believe I'm really here with you."

Catherine smiled and kissed him, but he gently pushed her away. "Be careful," he said. "Your father promised you to someone else."

She rolled her eyes. "He'll change his mind." She curled back into Sage's arms, and he happily wrapped his arms around her.

They had no idea they were being watched. A man stood among the trees. He was built like a bull, with a thick neck, small eyes, a pug nose, and nostrils that flared with fury.

I knew two things immediately: This man was Jamie, Catherine's betrothed . . . and this man was Ben. Magda's vision was a window into his heart, and I saw the terrible plan hatch from his hurt and anger. He'd accuse her of witchery. She'd be shamed, just like she was shaming him by taking up with another man when she was supposed to be his. That would teach her.

I wanted to scream to him not to do it, that things wouldn't go the way he expected, but I could only watch as the scene changed again.

Catherine was tied to the stake, flames licking at her feet. As the smoke rose around her, she saw Jamie in the crowd. He was pale and gaunt, as if he hadn't eaten or slept in weeks. He rocked back and forth muttering prayers, but it was too late to take back what he'd done. Catherine shook her head sadly, then sought out Sage in the crowd. He had her necklace clutched tightly in one fist. Five guards held him back, and he struggled against them, tears streaming down his face as he watched the fire grow.

I hadn't realized I wasn't breathing until the image changed again. I saw Anneline, the famous French actress. She and Sage had made it to their wedding day, and Sage had finally relaxed, positive that this time he had dodged tragedy.

I saw them at home, the picture of domestic bliss. Then a package arrived. Roses from an anonymous fan, just like the ones in my dream. I understood that this was only the latest in a long stream of bouquets. The attached notes had gone from sweet, to a little overbearing, to threatening. This one said, *If I can't have you, no one can*.

Sage threw a fit. He'd demanded help from the police, but he felt they'd done nothing. He was sure this man would kill Anneline.

She thought Sage was overreacting, but he grew so distraught that she caved. She agreed to put her career on hold for a while and get out of town. Sage warned her not to tell anyone where they were going, and she mostly listened. She told only a few of her closest lifelong friends about the bungalow in the Greek isles.

Julien was one of those friends. After a few months, he leaked Anneline and Sage's location to the newspapers for a large sum of money. I recognized Julien when I saw him . . . not only because he'd appeared in my dreams, but also, of course, because he was Ben.

With Julien's information, the stalker found Anneline and killed her with multiple stab wounds: one for each red rose he'd ever sent.

Then I saw Delia. She'd gotten involved with the notorious gangster Eddie because she thought he'd make her a star. Then Sage—the new piano player at the speakeasy—showed up. I could feel his turmoil. He didn't want to get involved with Delia. He didn't want another tragedy.

But he couldn't stay away.

He told himself that this time he'd find a way to change the story. This time he and Delia would live a long and happy life.

Though Delia and Sage's relationship was a secret, Delia had told her closest friend Richie. Richie worked for Eddie, and he tried to help her by fixing Eddie up with lots of other women, but Eddie caught on. He started watching Delia like a hawk, and when he finally caught her with Sage, he expressed his discontent with a single bullet between the eyes for both of them.

Sage could heal from this. Delia could not.

Richie, once again, was Ben.

"They're tied together, this man and your daughter, in a tragic circle that continues throughout eternity."

The voice was Magda's, but the image had shifted, and it was too dim to make out at first.

When it came into focus, I realized it was right here in this room, in Shibuya 109.

Magda was holding someone's hands . . . a man's hands . . .

Oh my God, they were my father's hands. I saw

him now, and he was so real that I thought I could reach out and hug him. It felt so good and hurt so much that my whole body ached.

Magda let go of him, and Dad opened his eyes. He looked pale and shaken, and I knew he'd seen the same visions we had. "He'll find her in this life," Magda said. "It will end the same."

"How do I stop it?" Dad asked desperately.

Magda smiled. "I thought you came here to find the Elixir of Life."

"That was before I knew. I don't care about all that. I want to save my daughter. I'll do whatever it takes."

"It will take Sage's final, irrevocable destruction. He must come for it willingly. All you can do is try to convince him."

"I'll do it," Dad said.

"*Without* telling him about me," Magda said. "I'd like that part to be a lovely surprise."

"Fine. Where do I find him?"

Magda's smile spread wider, and the image in my head changed again, to another spot I knew: Sage's house. Dad and Sage were talking, but Sage hadn't told us about this part of their conversation.

"Here are your options," Dad said. "Cursed Vengeance thinks they need to destroy you, but they don't know how. If they get you, your life will be nothing but torture as they try. The Saviors of Eternal Life see you only as a vessel for the Elixir. In their hands you'll live as a museum piece, displayed under lock and key. One of these groups will find you. It's only a matter of time."

"So you're offering death as an alternative," Sage said wryly. "I'm not sure I see the upside for me."

"I have one other thing that I very much hope will convince you," Dad said. He pulled out a picture of me and handed it to Sage. It was just a snapshot, nothing special, and nothing that featured a mysterious presence. "She's my daughter, Clea."

Sage looked at the picture, a little confused, and nodded, then handed it back. "She's lovely."

"You don't recognize her." Dad said. "Interesting. I think you would in person. You've met her before. Olivia was her name the first time."

The name hit Sage like a punch to the stomach. He was shaky and frightened . . . but also elated. His soulmate was alive and in the world again. It was only a matter of time before she would call to him, and he would find her. Could this time be different? Sage didn't know. Part of him didn't care. Just to be with her and be happy, even for a little while, even if it ended horribly . . .

No, that wasn't fair to her. He would find her, but it *wouldn't* end horribly. He wouldn't let it. He'd be vigilant this time, more vigilant than all the other times . . .

Dad saw Sage's thoughts in his eyes, and he shook his head sadly. "No, Sage. It won't end well. You'll be fine; you always are. But she won't. She'll die. Horribly and painfully."

Agony warped Sage's features. "You don't know that, not for sure. . . ."

"How many times are you going to let this happen?" Dad asked. "How many times are you going to rip this woman away from her life and everyone in it who loves her? You might be able to wait and get her back in another hundred years, but we lose her forever."

Sage pursed his lips and clenched his jaw. "So I'll stay away from her."

"You won't be able to. Don't you understand? There's only one way for Clea to live, and that's for you to break the circle. Let me take you to the Dark Lady. She can release you. The cycle will end. Please . . . if you truly love her, you'll do this."

Sage considered it. He wanted so badly to

hope, to try once more to find happiness with the woman he loved more than anything . . . but to see her—to see *me*—destroyed again . . . nothing was worth that. Not even his own life.

"I'll do it," he told Dad. "I'll go with you."

Finally Magda's hand slipped out of mine, snapping me back to reality so quickly I felt like I had the bends. I understood it all now, more than I wanted to understand. I knew why he ran when he first saw me, why he acted like he didn't really care. I knew why he pulled away after our night at the hotel.

"You didn't want to come here to find the Elixir at all," I accused Sage. "You came to kill yourself." I shook my head as the enormity of what I had seen continued to sink in. "He *asked* you to kill yourself."

"He was right," Sage said. "It's the only way to save you."

"It's true," Magda lilted. "The cycle will continue until the Elixir is properly returned to the universal powers that created it. That can only be done with a soul transfer. Sage . . . be a dear and tear open the canvas on the wall."

She looked toward an oil painting. Sage ripped the corner of the canvas and peeled it back to reveal a golden scabbard. The blade he pulled from it gleamed.

"Careful," warned Magda. "It's very sharp. It's made to rend not only flesh and bone, but also the soul."

"So that's all it takes," Sage said, eyeing the dagger. "Something so easy . . ."

"Not *that* easy," Magda cautioned. "There are considerations for the universe before it grants release. You must build a fire, and by its light you must demonstrate an understanding of your time here, and all the earthly pleasures you willingly sacrifice to set things right. At exactly midnight—this is the challenging part—you have to shove that blade into your heart. *You* have to do it—no looking for other willing volunteers."

"Enough," I said. "That's not going to happen."

"That's not your choice," Magda snapped, then turned back to Sage. "Do what I say, and your soul will be released. Your body will die, and the Elixir in it will be neutralized."

"I understand," Sage said. He tucked the dagger into his jacket.

"You don't, actually," Magda said. "I saved a couple of little details."

She sounded giddy. I wanted to smack her.

"When your soul is cut from your body like this, it can't get to the afterworld. It will try to find another host, an empty body. Those aren't usually lying around at just the right moment, I'm afraid, so instead your soul will whirl around in terribly painful suffering for a while, before ripping apart into nothingness." Magda smiled, then added, "What I'm saying is, it won't be fun for you."

"This isn't right," I said.

"Of course it is. Look at all the lives Sage has destroyed—including four of yours. Don't you think he should pay? Don't bother answering—it doesn't matter what you think. Sage knows the truth, and I take great pleasure in knowing he'll make the right choice." Magda turned her eyes to Sage, and for just a moment I saw a hint of youthful innocence in them.

"Good-bye, my love . . . it's time for me to rest." Her mouth spread in a wicked grin, and any innocence in her eyes was blotted out. "The kind of rest you'll never know."

With an impossible burst of strength, she whipped up her arm, ripped the chain from her neck, and hurled it to the ground, where the glass charm shattered.

Magda's paper-thin body dissolved into dust and disappeared.

thirteen

"CLEA, SAGE . . . ," Ben began, struggling for words. "I . . ."

Before he could finish, we heard loud scuffling above our heads.

"What is that?" I asked.

The noise grew, like a stampede. Sage looked grim. "Someone knows we're here."

"Then we should stay where we are," I said. "They won't find us here."

"They'll check the stairwells," Sage said. "And if they see the door, they'll come in. We'd be cornered."

"But if we leave, we could walk right into them," I countered.

"It's a big building. If we leave, we have a chance to escape," Sage said.

"Ben?" I asked.

Ben looked like he was a million miles away.

"Ben!"

"Clea . . ."

He looked pained. I got it; we'd both seen the same things, but we didn't have time to dwell on that right now.

"Snap out of it, Ben. We need you here."

The pounding was directly above us, and now I heard voices. I couldn't make out words, but it seemed like they might be in the stairwell and on their way down.

I turned to Sage. "You're right. We need to go."

We raced down the hall and climbed out the little door. The pounding feet and voices were getting closer. We ducked into the mall, anxiously falling in step with a crowd of shoppers. It was ten at night, so there weren't many, but there were enough. We walked quickly, trying to be cool and blend in until we could reach the doors.

"HEY!"

I looked up to see a man leaning over the escalator well two floors up. He started running after us as he reached for his walkie-talkie and shouted into it, "Targets spotted! Targets spotted! Heading for the exit!"

We broke into a run as several more men leaped out of stores and stairwells to join in the chase. They seemed to come from everywhere. They didn't wear uniforms, and they were a rainbow of nationalities, but it wasn't hard to pick them out. Every one of them looked hardened—hard muscles and hard souls, like unrepentant prisoners who'd had nothing to do for decades except lift weights and plan their revenge.

"Oh my God, they have guns!" Ben warned.

"Weave!" Sage shouted. "They're less likely to shoot if they can't get good aim!"

We ran side to side as we raced for the exit. I screamed as the first shot rang out and a store window shattered.

The few people left in the mall were in full panic mode now, screaming and diving for cover.

I heard two more shots before we made it outside. Sage raced for the curb, trying car door after car door until one opened.

"Get in!" he hollered. "And duck down!"

Ben slipped into the backseat, and Sage and I

took the front. We all ducked moments before we heard the riot of noise that had to mean our pursuers had emerged.

"What are we going to do, just hide here?" I whispered to Sage. "We might as well have stayed behind the little door!"

Sage didn't answer me. He was fidgeting with something under the dash. A second later the car roared to life. He clambered into the seat and drove off at top speed.

"You know how to hot-wire a car?" I asked.

"You learn a lot of things when you're around for five hundred years," he replied.

I climbed off the car floor and into my seat, scrambling for my seat belt. Behind me Ben did the same. I thought we'd gotten away . . . and then I heard a gunshot. I screamed and ducked down again.

"Shit!" Sage grimaced. "They're trying to shoot out our tires."

He pushed harder on the accelerator. There were too many cars and no room to move. He swerved into oncoming traffic.

Horns blasted.

"What are you doing?" I screamed.

"Hold on!" Sage cried. He swerved back into

the proper lane, avoiding a head-on collision by a nanosecond.

I closed my eyes, only for an instant. If I was going to die, I at least wanted to be aware of my last moments.

Sage maneuvered through a network of small and large streets, constantly weaving to dodge traffic. He laid on his horn as he raced through crosswalks and onto sidewalks, scattering pedestrians before he blew past.

"Ben, are you okay?" I looked back to check. He'd gone white. He couldn't even handle the teacups ride at Disney World. I could only hope he wouldn't lose it now.

He shook his head and curled tighter in his seat.

I lifted myself up to check behind us, but Sage pushed me back down. "Don't do that."

"I just want to know how many there are."

"Too many." Sage pushed the car to a breakneck pace, then screeched a U-ie and started twisting wildly through alleys, one hairpin turn after another.

I heard tires screeching, and a massive crash.

"WHOOOOO!" Sage laughed triumphantly. "Check it out!"

I spun around, and out the rear windshield I caught a glimpse of the steaming wreckage of two smashed cars receding into the distance. Other cars pulled around them, picking up the chase. I ducked back down into my seat.

"Not bad, right?" Sage asked.

He was grinning. The chase fueled him. Adrenaline lit up his eyes, and his muscles tensed as he pushed himself and the car to their limits.

I had never seen him look hotter. In a sick way, I kind of didn't want the chase to end.

"Hold on!" Sage cried. We were out of the alleys now. He raced the car to top speed before whirling a three-sixty, sending three more cars piling into one another.

Sage caught my eye. "Heart pounding yet?"

It was . . . and I got the sense that he knew exactly why. He smiled—then gunshots brought his attention back to the chase. I breathlessly watched him through several more minutes of death-defying driving until we'd lost every car that was after us.

We were speeding up a mostly clear expressway now, not a tail in sight.

"Um, Sage?" Ben finally said. He still looked sick, but the color had started to return to his face. "Where are we going?"

"Kujukuri Beach," he said. "About forty-five minutes away, and pretty secluded at this hour.

We'll stop for some wood and a lighter . . . put us there about eleven thirty."

Sage said it lightly, but I knew better. I wasn't surprised, but it still made my blood run cold.

"Really?" Ben asked. "Shouldn't we just stop somewhere and figure out our next move?"

Clearly, Ben was still thrown from everything that had happened. He didn't understand.

"Sage *has* figured out our next move," I said.

"Okay . . . what is it?"

"Release," Sage and I said at the same time.

"Release like . . . the dagger?" Ben asked.

"It's why we came," Sage said.

Ben opened his mouth, but he didn't object. Instead he looked at me and raised an eyebrow, asking for my reaction.

"It was his plan all along," I said.

And if all went according to Sage's plan, he'd be dead in almost exactly an hour and a half. I'd have thought that would be dramatic enough to spur a long conversation, filled with drawn-out good-byes and sad stories about what could have been. Instead we just sat in silence.

"You guys," Ben finally said, "I can't stop thinking about what we saw . . . what I did . . ."

"It wasn't you," I said.

"It was, though," he argued. "It was."

It *was*. It was him, and he'd done horrible things to me lifetime after lifetime.

"I betrayed you every time," Ben went on, "and what happened to you . . ."

He choked up, and I seized on the one thing in Magda's vision that made it a little better.

"You didn't ask for those things to happen," I said. "Remember? You didn't know how bad it would get."

"But that's worse! It means I can never trust myself. Even when I think I'm doing the right thing, I'm not."

He was right. Even when he was trying to help me, his actions always led to my death.

Would it happen again?

No. This was Ben. *My* Ben. Whatever he had been before, in this lifetime he'd die before he'd do anything to hurt me. I knew it absolutely.

Nagging doubt still itched at my brain, but I pushed it aside.

"What happened then doesn't have to happen now," I promised him. "Those people weren't you. They may be part of you, but they're not *you*."

"How can you be sure?" he asked. I could hear in his voice how badly he wanted to believe me.

"It's all part of the cycle," Sage said. "It ends tonight."

He pulled into a market.

"I'll just be a minute," he said.

"Can you leave me your phone?" I asked. "I need to text Rayna, let her know we're alive."

Sage raised his eyebrows at my choice of words, but he handed me the phone before heading into the market.

"I'll be right back," I told Ben, and slipped out of the car. I brought my camera case with me.

I had a plan.

I didn't text Rayna. Instead I reached into the case and pulled out the web address and pass code I'd found in my dad's office: the forum site for the Saviors of Eternal Life. I wrote quickly and simply who I was, that I was with Sage, and we were on our way to Kujukuri Beach. I said that if they wanted the Elixir, they had to get to us by midnight, or it would be too late.

Sage was already on his way back to the car. I didn't have time to look over the other posts on the site, to see if it had any recent activity. I could only throw the information out there and hope someone would come for us before it was too late.

I was reaching out to one of our worst enemies,

but it was my only option, and I felt like it could work. The only thing I could do now was wait.

"Rayna says hi," I said, handing Sage back the phone.

We climbed back into the car and continued on to the spot he'd chosen to end his own life.

We pulled up at Kujukuri Beach with about thirty minutes to go.

All three of us piled out of the car, but Sage put a hand on Ben's shoulder.

"If you don't mind . . . I'd like to be alone with Clea."

Ben looked hurt for a moment, then glanced back and forth between Sage and me. "Of course," he said.

The two guys stood awkwardly, well aware this would be the last time they'd see each other. Ben finally extended his hand. "I don't know what to say."

Sage considered Ben a moment, then took his hand and pulled him in for a hug. He whispered something in Ben's ear, and Ben nodded as they stepped apart.

Sage took my hand, and together we walked down the beach. It was long and wide, dotted by large dunes and set against a residential area that was fast asleep this time of night. We trekked down until we were around ten feet from the water, close enough for the sand to be solid and packed under our feet, but far enough that the waves wouldn't roll up and get in the way of Sage's plans.

I'd felt strong on the ride here. I didn't really let myself believe this was actually going to happen. I even had a plan to stop it.

But now we were really here, just a few minutes before midnight, and there was no guarantee my plan would work. If it didn't, it was over. It wasn't like I could wrestle the dagger away from Sage. If he wanted to do this, he would.

The tears welled up in my eyes, and I tried to keep my voice from cracking.

"What now?"

"I build a fire, like Magda said, and acknowledge all the earthly pleasures I'm sacrificing."

He took my hand and led me to a dry patch of sand, then pulled me into his arms for a long kiss.

That was it. I started sobbing.

"Don't do this," I begged him. "You don't have to."

"I do. Even your father knew it."

I couldn't speak. I was crying too hard for anything else to come out. Sage leaned in to kiss the top of my head. I saw tears in his eyes too. As he moved away I grabbed his hand and pulled him into my arms. I clung to him as the sobs tore through me. If I held on to him hard enough, he couldn't do any of it. He'd have to stay here with me until after midnight. I'd get one more day, and if I could get one, I could get more. I had to keep him with me, no matter what.

Gently but firmly, Sage pushed me away. Not having his arms around me was the most devastating feeling in the world. It felt like death. I plopped onto the sand, completely helpless and lost.

As I cried, Sage worked. He built and lit a small bonfire, surrounding it with drawings he etched into the sand with a twig. The end result was a circle of pictures illustrating his time on this earth . . . his time with me.

He came back to me and took my hand. I clutched it like a lifeline. He put his arm around me and I snuggled in as close as I could possibly get, memorizing the feeling of his body next to mine.

Sage walked me on a tour of our lives together, one image after another. Sage and Olivia in a rowboat on the Tiber. Sage and Catherine dancing in their favorite field. Sage and Anneline at the altar on their wedding day. Sage and Delia, smiling to each other over the piano. Sage and I on the beach in Rio, seeing each other for the very first time.

It was a work of art. *We* were a work of art. I didn't want to believe it could end.

I heard a sniffle and realized that Sage was crying too. I looked up at him and made him meet my eyes. "Don't do it," I demanded.

"I have to," he choked.

He forced his eyes away to glance down at his watch. "Eleven fifty-five," he said huskily. "You have to go. I don't want you to see this."

I stretched up and pressed my lips to his. I wrapped my arms tightly around his neck as we kissed. I willed it not to end. If I could keep him with me for just a little more than five minutes, we'd be fine.

Five minutes. It was all I needed.

Kissing him hungrily, I ran my hands over his body, down his chest, past the belt of his jeans. . . .

"No, Clea," he begged, pushing my hands off him. "I can't let you."

"You can. You want to. Please." I dove back into his arms and started kissing him again, frantic now, desperate to keep him occupied.

"No!"

He pushed me off him, hard, and I tumbled into the sand. He wiped away the last of his tears with the back of his hand, then pulled out the dagger. "I'm sorry, Clea, but I have to. I love you."

"I love you, too," I tried to say . . . but all that came out were sobs.

Sage checked his watch—did he even have another minute?

That was when I heard the screech of tires. Headlights flashed, and an old VW bus barreled onto the sand. The doors opened, and three men and two women poured out, each toting a gun.

My God, was it really them? I nearly fainted with relief, but there wasn't time for that. They weren't far, but they hadn't seen us yet.

"Here! Right here!" I screamed, waving my arms.

Five guns wheeled and pointed right at me.

"What are you doing?" Sage cried.

"Over here!" I screamed again.

"Clea!" Sage roared, and dove, throwing himself on top of me as the group of five Saviors of Eternal Life opened fire and ran toward us. They knew the shots would only stop Sage, not kill him, and they didn't care what happened to me. Sage kept me low, and pulled us behind a protective dune.

"What did you do?" he hissed.

"Told them where we were. I didn't have any other choice."

The shots were closer now. Sage grabbed my hand and ran with me, weaving down the beach and ducking behind the dunes. We raced as fast as we could. The effort tore at my lungs, but I welcomed the pain. Sage was with me. He was alive.

A monstrous pain seared through my body and I fell to the ground behind a sand dune. I grabbed my thigh. It was gushing blood. My head started to swim.

"Clea!" Sage dropped to his knees and pressed on my leg, trying to stop the blood.

"Clea!" another voice screamed.

Ben? I saw him racing down the beach toward us. No, no! Bad idea. I wanted to scream at him to get back, get away, but that would only get the Saviors' attention.

"Clea! Clea!" Ben cried as he ran blindly through the dunes.

Shit! He didn't need my help getting their attention. They saw him now, saw him barreling toward us. It wouldn't take a genius to realize we were together. Summoning my strength and hoping to distract the shooters for even a moment, I screamed out, "Ben, stop! Get away! Get out of here!"

Too late. A male shooter grabbed him and held him tight, and the group huddled around him.

"We have your friend!" one of the women cried. "Give us what we want and we won't hurt him."

Give them what they want? Give them Sage? No! I swung to face him. He smiled tenderly and brushed my hair behind my ear.

"How's your leg? Is it okay?"

"Don't, Sage. . . ."

"It's just grazed. I know it hurts. You're going to be fine."

Panic swelled inside me, and I gripped his shirt, hard. "Don't go."

"He's nothing to them, Clea. They'll hurt him if I don't."

I didn't care. I didn't want Ben to be hurt, but I didn't want Sage to leave even more. "No." It was the only word I could say. "No, no, no, no, no."

Sage silenced me with a kiss, then disentangled my fingers from his shirt and walked up the beach toward Ben and the group, his hands raised in surrender.

"It's a deal," Sage said calmly. "Me for him. Let him go."

"No," Ben said weakly, but there was nothing he could do. The woman grinned, then nodded to the man holding Ben. The man pushed Ben roughly away, and he staggered toward Sage. Sage helped Ben steady himself for a moment. They spoke for just a second before two more men swooped down and grabbed Sage, holding their guns to his temples. They rushed him into the van, and the door slammed closed as it sped off.

Sage was gone. I stared at the spot where the van had disappeared.

Sirens pierced the night, and lights flashed in the distance. Police cars.

"Clea," Ben began. He was next to me now, and tried to reach for me, but I pushed him away.

"Do you hear that?" I shouted. "The police! Five more minutes! That's all we needed! All you had to do was stay where you were! Sage would be here and alive!"

"Oh God, I know," Ben said miserably. "I know . . . but I saw you go down and I had to get to you, and . . . I did it again. I messed everything up."

Ben started to sob. Normally I'd be the first to comfort him, but I was numb.

The sirens grew louder as the police cruisers pulled up next to us on the beach. They would have been right on time, but now it was too late.

I spent the next hours disconnected from everything. The police said they'd gone to the beach because neighbors heard gunshots. They interviewed Ben and me, and we said we didn't know anything about the shooters. We were just out for a walk when they opened fire.

They took me to the hospital to have my leg examined and I sat in the emergency room for what seemed like forever. People were all around, but they spoke Japanese and I couldn't understand a word. It blended into a dull background roar. Ben tried to talk to me, but I couldn't. When they finally called my name, it was a relief to leave him in the waiting room. My nurse spoke English, and told me I was lucky—I only had a flesh wound. She was wrong, but my other wounds weren't anything she could see.

There was something soothing about the examining room. It was so white and clean—sitting there made me feel like I was outside the real world, and I could pretend the last day hadn't happened. I imagined Sage, not Ben, was waiting for me outside. I wanted to stay longer, but I couldn't. They gave me crutches and sent me on my way.

When I came out, Ben had a taxi waiting. He'd arranged a flight back home, and we had to get to the airport right away. I felt like I was swept along, and didn't have a chance to think until we were in the air. Ben sat next to me. He was trying so hard. He'd bought us tickets in first class so I could stretch out my leg, and asked the flight attendant for extra pillows so I could prop it up.

"Are you comfortable?" he asked. "I can get another pillow."

"I'm fine."

"Are you sure?"

"I'm sure."

It had now been eight hours since they'd taken Sage. The Saviors had him . . . but for how long? He had the dagger with him. Any night at midnight he could kill himself, and I'd never even know.

I felt completely lost. How had it come to this? Could I have stopped it? I went over and over it in my head, but I always came back to the same thing.

Ben.

If Ben hadn't come running down that hill . . .

It might not have been fair—it wasn't fair—but that was how I felt.

I squirmed in my seat.

"Is your leg bothering you?" Ben asked. "Can I get you something?"

"It's not my leg that hurts," I said.

Ben opened his mouth to say something, then thought better of it. He reached up and tugged at his front tuft of hair and sighed.

Even the sigh was asking too much of me. I didn't want to hear it. I turned away and curled up as if I were going to sleep. I wondered if I actually could. I was exhausted, and it might be the perfect escape . . . but I was afraid. To have him in my dreams and then wake up . . . I'd lose him all over again. I couldn't bear it.

Even worse was the thought that I could close my eyes and he wouldn't be there at all.

Ben sighed again. It was like nails down a chalkboard. I got up and struggled down the aisle to the bathroom. I could see Ben dying to jump up and help me, but he knew better.

Inside, I stared at my face in the mirror. It didn't look like me. I wondered when it had happened. When had I changed so completely inside that I couldn't even recognize myself?

I had a sudden feeling that this stranger could have a world of secrets to share.

Maybe I just needed to listen.

I tried.

Nothing.

I leaned forward, staring into her eyes.

I looked away and went back to my seat.

Whatever she had to say, I couldn't hear it.

I didn't know if I ever would.

acknowledgments

MY HEARTFELT THANKS to the many people who helped bring *Elixir* to life. It has been an exciting challenge to write my first book, and I appreciate the people in my life who encouraged me to do it.

First, a big thanks to Elise Allen, my smart and nimble collaborator. You taught me so much during this process. Your positive attitude and zest for storytelling kept me inspired and driven even on those nights we worked tirelessly until three in the morning obsessing over a pesky "and" or "the."

To my editor, Emily Meehan, her assistant, Julia Maguire, and the team at Simon & Schuster who shared my excitement for this book from the first time we met, and followed through with such enthusiasm: Carolyn Reidy, Jon Anderson, Justin Chanda, Anne Zafian, Paul Crichton, Nicole Russo, Elke Villa, Jenica Nasworthy, Felix Gregorio, Chava Wolin, Lizzy Bromley, and Tom Daly.

To my literary agents, Fonda Snyder and Rob Weisbach, who gave me confidence and expertly helped guide me through this new venture.

Mom, THANK YOU. You have always encouraged me to step outside my comfort zone and challenge myself! Thanks for teaching me persistence and dedication. You always remind me to reach as high as I can!

Mike, thank you for patiently listening to my constant blabbering and ideas about Sage and Clea as their story was being born. I love you!

Ry-ry, thanks for keeping my life on track during this very busy time and for always bringing the comic relief.

My MOST IMPORTANT thanks go to my extremely supportive, dedicated, and loyal fans. The epic amount of love that you continue to show means everything to me! I truly hope you enjoy the book!